Chasing Dreams

Alison Mello

Chasing Dreams

 LIMITLESS
PUBLISHING

Limitless Publishing, LLC
Kailua, HI 96734
www.limitlesspublishing.com

Formatting: Limitless Publishing

ISBN-13: 978-1-68058-561-2
ISBN-10: 1-68058-561-4

Chapter 1

Skyler

"Sky, are you coming out tonight?" Sadie whines at me as she heads into her room to get some clothes together.

"I don't know." I roll my eyes because we go through this every time I have a weekend off.

"Listen, you have been in LA for two years now, you got yourself a job, and you've been landing some decent gigs at a few different clubs. It's time to land you a man."

I laugh at her because she knows full well every time I hook up with someone, it's either a one-night stand or if I give them a chance, I sabotage the relationship because I'm not happy.

I moved to LA two years ago to chase my dream of a singing career and met Sadie when I came across her ad in the local newspaper. She was looking for a roommate, because the girl she had been living with moved out to live with her boyfriend. I called her up, and we met at a local

1

coffee house. We hit it off and have been best friends ever since.

I've tried dating a few men since living here, and because they are so damn boring sexually or they're simply assholes, I end up cheating on them or just stop calling them.

"Sadie, I'm a barmaid and I sing in bars, so I don't know if I feel like hanging in another bar."

Sadie rolls her eyes at my lame ass excuse. "I get that, but Jonah said the club is kicking ass now that some new owner has taken over. He's working the door tonight so we get in for free."

"Cool, so we save what, like ten bucks?" I say with total sarcasm.

Sadie laughs and launches a pillow around the corner. It slams me right in the face.

"Real mature, Sadie!" I yell from my spot on the couch.

"It's about time you have a night with something other than that battery-operated boyfriend of you yours, and besides, Jonah says the new owner is single."

I burst out laughing, first because she brought up my battery-operated boyfriend and second because the truth comes out. "Ah, so truth be told, you're hoping we will bump into the owner so you can try to hook me up?"

"Only with a new singing gig." Sadie winks at me and heads to the bathroom to jump in the shower. "Go pick out your clothes. You're coming out tonight!" she yells from behind the bathroom door.

"At least B.O.B doesn't drag me out of the house

on my night off!" I yell back, knowing full well she probably can't hear me and couldn't care less about what I have to say.

I climb off the couch with a grunt and head to my bedroom in search of something to wear. I settle on a pair of jeggings with a tank top and a pink off the shoulder fitted tunic top. I start looking for some jewelry to wear when I come across my mom's wedding ring, and I'm tempted to put it on so no one will hit on me tonight but I know Sadie will give me shit so I leave it there. I smile, thinking about my mom, and it makes me realize how much I miss her.

My parents were in a serious, fatal car accident a few months before I moved out to LA. Being an only child, there was nothing keeping me on the East Coast. It was time to shoot for my dream of becoming a singer, so I sold most of my belongings and what couldn't be sold I donated. I sold my parents' house, taking the money from the sale and whatever I had in savings, along with my clothes, and flew out west in search of a new life. I met Sadie, and now I have some great friends thanks to her. She got me the job as a barmaid at Dugan's, the local bar, in between singing gigs.

Sadie comes out of the bathroom wrapped in nothing but a towel with her hair dripping wet.

"What are you doing?"

"Shelly is meeting us at the club with Rick."

"Okay, cool. I'm going to jump in the shower."

Sadie can be such a pain in my ass, but I love her dearly. She's a great friend and an incredible artist. She's been busting her tail to get her artwork into some of the bigger galleries here in LA. She says it's all displayed in smaller art galleries and that isn't good enough. I guess I can understand that. It would be like me saying I have some singing gigs at local clubs, so I don't need to shoot for the big recording deal I want. We all want to be the best at what we do in life and we all want to be noticed; it's all about how hard we're willing to work at it. I'm willing to work pretty hard.

I get out of the shower and quickly dry up before I wrap my hair in a towel and throw on my robe. Unlike my roommate, I actually own a robe. Sadie chooses to walk around half naked, and I can now honestly say my lack of being happy with the men I have slept with has nothing to do with my sexual preference. Sadie is gorgeous and I have seen her naked more times than you can imagine. I still have no desire to switch teams.

I'm standing in front of our full-length mirror checking out my clothes and making sure I look okay when Sadie comes to stand next to me.

"You look hot, girl."

I have flat ironed my light brown hair to perfection and done my eye makeup in a smoky gray and pink blend. I'm wearing my favorite jeans. I love them because they make my ass look amazing. Sadie slaps me hard and tells me she wishes she had an ass as good as mine.

"Oww." I rub my now throbbing ass. "Oh please, girl, you have the most gorgeous blonde hair and your blue eyes are so bold and beautiful. And don't act like you don't have a killer body."

She runs her fingers through her hair. "Yeah, but

you have great boobs *and* an ass. I'm pretty flat in both those areas. Plus you have some killer brown eyes."

I look back at the mirror to my perky boobs, thankful I'm pretty equally proportioned. I also stand at 5'7" compared to her 5'4". I smile and walk away from the mirror feeling pretty confident.

When we get to the club, I notice as we are walking from the parking lot it's now named Club Thrive and has a pretty slick new sign outside. I give Sadie a questioning look. She gives me a sideways grin and raises her eyebrows. "Wait until you see the inside. It has been redone."

We approach the front of the very long line and find Jonah standing there.

"Good evening, ladies," he says in his deep voice, moving the red rope. We walk on in while everyone at the door grunts and groans because they have to wait. Jonah gives Sadie a quick kiss before he takes his place back at the door. They are so adorable together. He towers over her, but they make a cute couple. He's a really big guy with broad shoulders and huge arms. He acts rough and tough, but Sadie says he's a big teddy bear.

***

Logan

Jonah's girlfriend Sadie is heading over to the bar with a friend, who is absolutely stunning. They snag two seats that just cleared out, and I shout, "Hey, Sadie!"

"'Sup, Logan?" She looks happy to see me.

"Are you going to introduce me to your friend?"

"Sure. Logan, this is Skyler. Skyler, this is Logan."

I give her a full-on smile. "How's it going, Skyler?"

"Good." She looks down, fighting a smile. It makes me think I got me a shy girl on my hands, and I think it's cute as hell.

I wipe the bar in front of them and ask, "What can I get you two gorgeous ladies tonight?"

"Can I get a Blue Hawaiian?" Skyler asks, finally showing me her gorgeous smile. She really is pretty.

"Sure thing."

"And I'll have a Sex on the Beach!" Sadie shouts over the music.

"Be right back, ladies." I walk away to make their drinks, realizing my night just got a hell of a lot better, though I wish they had come in on a night when it wasn't so busy or I wasn't stuck behind the bar so I could actually talk to Skyler. With Kelly, the regular bartender, out sick, there's no way I'll get away to find out what her deal is.

I glance over and they are giggling and laughing. I would give anything to know what they are talking about but can't hang around to find out because I have more drinks to make if I want to make some money tonight. This is the first time since I bought the place that I have gotten stuck behind the bar, so this is my chance to show my crew I'm not afraid to get my hands dirty.

I get back with their drinks, and I notice she's all

but staring at me. Hopefully I affect her as much as she affects me. Two more of her friends are approaching, so I stick around to take their order, and once I get back with the drinks, I tell her, "I'll check on you in a little bit." I look her in the eye and give her a wink before I walk away.

This place is so jammed it feels like forever until I can get to them again, but I keep an eye on their drinks because I don't want Shane to beat me to them. They're in the middle of the bar so it would be either of us serving them. Once I see their glasses are about empty, I head over.

"Can I get you all another round?"

Sadie laughs. "Yeah, same drinks please."

When I get back with their drinks, Skyler and Sadie are switching places with their friends. They all take sips of their drinks and Sadie shouts, "We're going to dance! He'll save our seats and drinks."

They all head to the dance floor.

***

Skyler

"Sadie, he is seriously fucking hot. Why didn't you tell me the bartender was amazing eye candy?"

She shrugs. "He doesn't usually bartend."

I narrow my eyes at her. "What do you mean he doesn't usually bartend? You clearly know him from hanging here with Jonah."

"He's the new owner I was telling you about."

I turn beet red. "Fuck me."

7

She bursts out laughing. "I'm pretty sure from the look on his face he would love the chance to."

He *is* incredibly sexy with his neatly kept dark hair and his big chocolate brown eyes. He's muscular without being overly bulky, and his hair is short on the sides but slightly long on top, brushed back with a slight wave to it. I look over to the bar and I swear he's watching us dance. I smile, hoping he sees me. I'm a bit braver now that I have some liquid courage in me. He smiles but I can't tell if it's at me or someone that he's making a drink for at the bar. Secretly I hope it's me, but I won't admit that to Sadie yet.

We've spent the entire night drinking and dancing. Well, Sadie does the drinking. I only have a couple because I have to drive us home. I know Sadie well enough to know that even if she says she'll drive home she won't. I've had a few guys try to dance with me, but I shake them off because I can't stop think about Logan and his killer smile. Sadie has to be wrong. There's no way a guy that hot is single, and if he is, there has to be something wrong with him.

It's now almost closing time and people are starting to leave. We're sticking around because Jonah has to close and he's going to walk us to our car after he's done. Once they are done emptying the place out the employees all get a drink on the house, so we will have a drink with him before we head home.

The music is finally off but we are all still talking loud from having to talk over the music for so long. It makes us all laugh, and we try to turn it

8

down a notch. Jonah comes over to the bar with a few other bouncers. Logan and the other bartender serve them up a round of drinks before they start cleaning up the rest of the glasses from the night. There isn't much because they kicked ass cleaning after last call, but they're still not done for the night.

Everyone's talking and having a good time. I find out that the other bartender working with Logan is Shane. Logan's only behind the bar because someone else called out sick. Jonah, Patrick, Trey, and Paul are the bouncers that stayed behind for drinks and are now hanging out with us.

Logan comes over about thirty minutes later and tells us he wants to lock up in about fifteen minutes so he wants us to finish up. I flash him a smile, and his gorgeous chocolate brown eyes lock with mine.

"You okay to get home?" he asks me.

"I cut myself off a while ago so I can get us home. We're roommates." I want to say 'why, you want to drive me?' but I don't have the nerve so I look down shyly instead.

Club Thrive may not be such a bad place to hang after all, especially if I get to check him out.

Chapter 2

Logan

I walk into the club ready to look over my inventory reports so I can order the liquor we are going to need. All I can think about is Skyler. Though she doesn't realize it, I watched her dance every chance I got last night. She has the most beautiful smile and an ass that any man would love to get their hands on. I noted that she wasn't dancing with any men either. Every time someone approached her, she brushed them off and continued dancing with her girls. I even dreamed about her shaking that amazing ass of hers on the dance floor, though this time she was dancing with me rubbing it against my throbbing cock.

I shake my head. I need to talk to Jonah as soon as he gets here so I can find out what her deal is. I almost asked her to dinner last night but was too worried she'd turn me down in front of everyone. I'll shoot him a text.

Logan: Hey can you see me in my office when you get here?

Jonah: Sure, is everything good?

Logan: Yeah we're good, man. I just need to talk to you.

Jonah: Cool, see you in a bit.

How sad am I? I have owned this club for about six months and I texted one of my bouncers to get the scoop on his girlfriend's friend.

I pull out my report and head into the back so I can see what we have in comparison to my report. I'm going through when I notice we are missing one bottle of rum, one bottle of vodka, and one bottle of Crown Royal. Now one bottle missing, okay, maybe it broke. One bottle of three different things missing and no one told me they broke anything seems suspicious to me.

I make a list of the things we need for the bar and add wine to the list. I want to see if we serve some nice wine if people will order it. I want the club to have a nice image, and nothing says nice like bottles of wine and champagne. I order some to sell by the bottle and some by the glass. I can't help but think about the fact that I may have a thief working for me and it's pissing me off, so I walk back to my office to think about how I'm going to catch this thief and what I'll do when I do catch the person. I'm finishing up placing the order when there is a knock on my office door. "Come in!" I shout in a bad mood.

"Hey, Logan, you wanted to see me?"

I rub my forehead and ask Jonah to come in and shut the door.

"'Sup, man? You look pissed."

"I am but that isn't why I texted you. Jonah, I think you're pretty loyal to me and the club, so I'm going to trust you because I need some help and then I'll tell you why I texted you."

"I think you have done good things with the club and I love bouncing, so if you're worried about me you can stop. Just tell me what's up."

"I think someone's stealing alcohol from the club. I'm missing some rum, vodka, and Crown Royal and I need to figure out how to catch them so I can fire their ass and make it known you don't steal from me."

"Who has access to the back room?"

"The seven bartenders do, Troy, my assistant manager, and me. I'm going to have to cut access to two bartenders a night, as well as me and Troy."

"I've never run a bar, but isn't there a sheet that they have to sign out what they took and for which bar?"

I raise my eyebrows in surprise. "Hey, that's a good idea. I'm creating something right now and revoking keys. I'll have to issue them out as the bartenders are on, so I can keep an eye on the room."

"I'll keep my eyes open and let you know if I see anything shady," Jonah tells me.

"Thanks, man. On a way better note, what's up with that hottie Skyler that came in with your girl?"

He bursts out laughing. "Dude, you texted me to hook you up with my girl's roommate?"

I grin. "Yup."

"I don't know. She's a pretty girl and she's sweet, but she has serious commitment issues."

"Maybe she hasn't found the right man yet."

"Maybe. I can hook you up and I know Sadie will be stoked. She's dying to get her a boyfriend, but watch your back."

He sounds leery, like I'm his little brother, and I can't help but laugh.

"I'll ask her out. I just want to know what her deal is. I'm a big boy. I can handle that part."

He laughs. "I don't know a ton other than she's from the East Coast, her parents died in a car crash, and since she had no family she moved out here trying to nail a career as a singer."

"How long has she been out here?"

"I've been with Sadie about a year and a half, and I know she had already been here a while, so probably at least two years."

"What does she do besides sing? I assume if she's hanging in nightclubs she's not famous and must do something else."

"Sadie got her a job a Dugan's, so she works there in between gigs."

"That shitty bar? I should give her a job here."

He shrugs.

"Alright, listen guy. I want you bouncing in the club tonight and anything shady you come straight to me. Got it?"

"You got it." Jonah gets up and shakes my hand, then leaves my office.

I send an email out to all of my bar staff saying there is a last minute mandatory meeting that everyone needs to be at by 8:00 pm and they are only excused if they text me and I excuse them. My phone pings a minute later and it's Kelly, the bartender who called out sick yesterday.

Kelly: Still sick, Logan.

Logan: What is wrong with you?

Kelly: I have a bad head cold and a headache.

Logan: Call me.

My phone rings a second later, which tells me she probably isn't faking it.

"Hey, Kelly," I answer, trying not to sound pissed.

"Hey, Logan, what's up?" She sounds like shit.

"To be honest, there are some issues here and I'm learning who I can trust and who I can't. Anyone can call out sick over text but it's hard to fake over the phone. You've just earned a little trust."

She's coughing and it sounds awful. "Sorry I'm so sick. I promise I'm trying to get better. I can't afford to miss another shift."

Kelly's trying to put herself through college so I understand she can't afford to miss a shift. Still, college is also the time when kids her age want to party. I think I have confirmed that she actually is sick and not trying to pull a fast one on me.

"I understand. Go rest and I'll see you in here next week. You're off until Wednesday night."

She sighs. "Thanks, Logan."

"See ya Wednesday," I say before I cut the call. I really like her. She's pretty hard working and easy on the eyes for the patrons.

I get no other texts so I go about preparing a sign out sheet. It'll be mandatory that they'll use it whenever they go in for fresh bottles. I'll be checking the inventory before every opening until I find out if someone is stealing and I can trust my staff. Then I'll be able to back off.

***

I have six bartenders in front of me. I plan to be brutally honest. I want to see their reactions when I tell them I think we may have a thief among us.

"We're all meeting here tonight because there are going to be some changes in the way we run the two bars in this club. It appears quite a few bottles of liquor have gone missing. If I find out someone is stealing alcohol from my club, you'll be fired immediately and I'll be sure to blacklist you from the remaining top clubs in the area. I expect trust and loyalty from my employees. Thieves cannot be trusted and they'll be dealt with."

I look around for a minute while everyone is looking at everyone else. My assistant manager is standing at my side with a slight grin on his face. I instantly wonder if it's him and he's enjoying that I think it's one of my bartenders. I'm glad he doesn't realize I've caught his grinning.

"Okay, so here's the deal. Troy and I'll have keys since one or both of us is here each night of the week. We can run liquor for you. On the busy nights, there will be two bartenders at each bar and one floater. The floater will have a key and will run alcohol, as well as bounce between the two bars to help out whichever is busier. As usual, tips will be split evenly so your runner doesn't get screwed. Any questions so far?"

I look around the room.

"You all have ear wigs, so if your runner is busy at another bar and you need something or your bar is overloaded and the runner is at the other bar helping, you'll call for Troy or me. We are both bartender certified and can pitch in. I worked the bar last night in Kelly's absence with Shane, and I had no issues getting my hands dirty."

They start grunting and mumbling things to each other. Some are even snickering.

"Guys, he seriously kicked ass," says Shane. "He didn't stop all night. I can't speak for Troy because I haven't worked the bar with him, but Logan held his own and he had some odd requests." He looks over to Troy. "Sorry, man!" Clearly I still have some respect to earn, as does Troy.

"Starting tonight, there will be this binder in the back room by the door. Anyone with a key that removes alcohol is to sign the bottle out with their name and the bar it's heading to. If a bottle breaks because you or another bartender dropped it, you're to sign it out and write down who reported the broken bottle. Do not start breaking too many bottles of alcohol. It's expensive and we'll have a whole new set of problems. Am I clear?"

I hear a bunch of grumbles and heads nodding.

"Troy, I want you behind the bar helping out this weekend. Show the team what you've got. Unless you have questions, I'm good for tonight. Your shifts for the week are posted, and if you need to, feel free to see me on the side."

The meeting concludes with everyone talking at once.

"Shane, can I see you a second?" I call.

He walks over right away. "Thanks. I know respect is earned in this business, and you helped me earn some." I shake his hand. "I owe you one."

"You earned it just keep the shifts coming, Logan. I think Troy is going to have issues though. I've been told he tries to be too much of a hard ass so he's never going to earn the respect of these people. We all work hard and he tries to call us on stupid shit if he doesn't like you. Like, 'That was too much vodka for that drink.' He told one of the guys who has been bartending for years that he needed to water them down more. It's your bar. Are we making drinks or serving punch?"

"Thanks for the heads up. We are definitely making drinks. I'll keep an eye on it and handle it, okay?"

"Cool," he says as he walks away from me.

After the bartenders who are not working tonight clear out, I head over to Troy, handing him the binder.

"I have an errand to run," I tell him. "I'll be back before we open. See this gets put in the back where it belongs and that everyone's using it."

He nods. "You got it, man."

"Oh, and the drawers for the night are set up in the back, so be sure to place them at the bar registers."

He nods and heads toward the back. My gut tells me it's my own assistant manager that I can't trust, and it pisses me off.

I head over to Dugan's for a beer, hoping Skyler is working. I pull up outside the bar and there are a few cars there but not too many. I wish I knew if one of them was Skyler's, but I have no idea what she drives. I pull open the door and walk inside. I've never been in this place before. It's dark like a typical sports bar, with sports decor all over the walls. There are a few strategically placed TVs playing news on one and sports on the others. I approach the bar, and the bartender turns around and gives me the most beautiful smile. It's her.

"Hey, Logan, what are you doing here?"

She looks cute in her uniform, but it doesn't do her justice. It's a sports polo with the bar logo and snug jeans that hug her amazing ass. The manager should let her pick her own clothes. He would have way more guys in here buying beers so they can drool over her amazing body.

"Isn't it obvious?"

"No, not to me. You own a club, so clearly you can get beer there."

I give her a cocky smile. "I guess that means I'm here to see you."

She blushes, holding up her finger telling me one minute when someone at the other end of the bar needs a drink. She quickly gives him another draft beer and heads back to my end of the bar.

"So did Jonah tell you I work here? And what can I do for you, Logan?"

"To answer your first question yes, and you can start with a scotch on the rocks."

Once she returns with it I thank her.

"So…what can I do for you?"

"You can have dinner with me Monday night."

She actually blushes more and looks down at the floor. "I don't know, Logan, I'm not good at the relationship thing and you seem like a nice guy."

"So what, you're afraid you're going to hurt me? I'm a big boy, Skyler. I can handle it."

She looks me in the eye. "My friends call me Sky."

I actually laugh. "Oh good, so we're friends now. That means we can have dinner as friends, right?"

"Yeah, I guess so. Where do you want to go?" She's having a hard time looking at me and it's killing me because she has the most killer brown eyes I have ever seen.

"Do you have your phone on you?" She pulls it from her back pocket and hands it to me. I send myself a text from her phone so I have her number and she has mine.

"I'll text you and we can decide where we want to go."

"Hey, Skyler, can I get a beer when you're done flirting with lover boy?" a guy shouts from the other end of the bar.

I shout back, "Sorry, man, can you blame me?"

He laughs. "Not at all. I wish I weren't double her age or I would flirt too."

Sky runs to get him another beer, her face fully flushed. I think it looks sexy on her. She knows what everyone is drinking so they must all be regulars.

I tell her I have to go, hand her a twenty for the drink, and leave before she can return with my change. She probably makes shit tips in this bar. I wanted to leave her a hundred but didn't want to insult her. I wonder if I should do a classy night at the club to go with the wine and I can have her sing. I guess I should find out how well she sings and what kind of music she sings first. Maybe Wednesday nights, I'll have to come up with a catchy name and figure out how to promote it. Maybe I can do a classy singles night with wine and cheese and cracker trays. Charge a cover fee that would be enough for the food and they would buy the liquor. I walk back to my car with a grin on my face. I would at least be able to see her every Wednesday. I shake my head, realizing how ridiculous I sound.

I walk back into my club, which will be opening soon, so my staff is busy getting things ready for a busy night.

"Hey, Kyle, where's Troy?"

He shrugs. "I haven't seen him."

I walk to the back in search of him and find him in the back room looking over bottles.

"What's up?"

He jumps. "Nothing, just checking inventory."

I give him a questioning look. "That's not your job. Did you do what I asked you to do?"

He nods toward the binder on the shelf by the

door. "I thought I would help with making sure everything is here."

"Did you put the cash drawers out yet?" He shakes his head. "Get on it."

I walk over to the log to see what has been signed out and by whom, then I head off to question that they actually took it, making sure they realize I'm doing it for reasons other than lack of trusting them. I also tell them to count their cash drawer before we open and be sure everything is there. I want to be sure he's not taking cash from me too. We have only had one drawer come up short and the bartender admitted to fucking up, so I let it go since it was only twenty bucks.

The night goes smoothly. I'm walking around while my staff is cleaning up and getting ready to close. I'm waiting to see if anyone complains about Troy helping at the bar. Everyone seemed to have the correct amount in their drawers and I'll double check the inventory tomorrow to make sure it matches where we should be for a Saturday night. I only had to come out and help a few times, which is a good thing because it gave me time to think about my plan for Singles Night. I'm torn over doing it on a Wednesday or a Sunday. They're both slow nights and could use some beefing up. Maybe I'll give my staff a chance to give me their input and see what they think. We're closed Mondays and Tuesdays, and right now I want to keep it that way a little longer. I think being a club versus a bar we don't need to open those nights; maybe in the future I can use those nights to rent it out for parties. Wednesday is 18+ night during the summer months, but since summer is coming to an end, I'll need something else to sustain us through the winter.

Everyone is sitting around having their drink on me for the night.

"Nice job tonight, everyone! I was able to get some work done in my office because you all busted tail and worked hard. I only had to come out a couple of times to help out and I appreciate it." They all cheer, hoot and holler. I laugh. "Okay, listen up. I have a question for you all before I kick you out so I can lock up and go home." There is more laughter. "I'm thinking about doing a Singles Night to replace the 18+ crowd as summer comes to an end. We will still have a cover charge but it will be a little higher and I'll have a fruit, cheese and cracker table that will be included and we will have wine available soon so customers can purchase that in place of other alcohol." I see a lot of nodding.

"I want us to be known as a classy place as well as a fun place to hang. I'm also thinking of having some classy live entertainment in place of a DJ. The problem is I can't decide if I should do Wednesday night or Sunday night. I'm thinking Wednesday night from 7:00-11:00 so it isn't too late for those who have to work early the next day but still gives us an event on that night. If you agree raise your hand."

I see a bunch of hands go in the air, and everyone looks excited.

"So you know, the staff will be required to wear button down shirts on that night with nicer pants, no jeans or polo shirts. Ladies, we can talk about what will work for you behind the bar, but we will have to look the part. If you do not want to be a part of this because of dress code or any other reason let me know and I'll schedule you accordingly. If Singles Night takes off, I'll move 18+ night to Sundays when summer rolls around again. I would like an email from anyone who doesn't want to work the Singles Night, and if I don't hear from you I'll assume you all want to be a part of it and will rotate you through. Now, everyone go home and I'll finish cleaning up. Great job tonight everyone!"

They all clear out while I clean up the remainder of the bar and put the glasses in the dishwasher. I throw the dishtowel on the bar and start thinking of Skyler, so I text her. I have no idea how late she had to work but it's totally possible she's still up.

Logan: Hey are you awake?

A minute later my phone pings.

Skyler: Yeah I just got home. Are you still at work?

Logan: Yeah. I'm getting ready to lock up and was thinking about dinner with you on Monday.

Skyler: :-) Where do you want to go?

Logan: Somewhere that we can talk and have conversation but that the food is still good.

Skyler: I like Trisha's diner, it's quiet and she has good food.

I stop and think for a second. I wanted to take her somewhere nicer but I want her to be comfortable too.

Logan: Okay Trisha's it is. How's 6:00?

Skyler: Six is fine with me. I'm off so I have no plans.

Logan: Cool, see you then, have a good night.

Skyler: You too!

I lock up and head home to get some sleep.

Chapter 3

Skyler

Sadie climbs on my bed.

"Hey, sleepy head, I know you worked last night but you might want to get up. You have a hot date tonight!"

I stretch, looking at my best friend lying on the side of me. I'm so tired. I didn't get home until two o'clock this morning and it always takes me a little while to fall asleep.

"You know you're the only female I would allow to lay in my bed with me, right?"

She bursts into laughter. "I feel so privileged."

"Oh shut up, and it's not a date. We're going out as friends."

She gives me a look that screams 'really?' "Logan wants you. He's thinking of this as a date even if you aren't."

"Well he was the one who said something like since we are friends, then we can have dinner because friends do dinner."

25

"Sky, I love you, but you have a lot to learn about men. He said that so you would agree to dinner. He wants to date you, and I don't know what your problem is. He's hot as hell, he owns his own club, and he's incredibly smart." She props herself up on her elbow.

"I told him I'm not good at relationships." I shake my head. "I'm hopeless. I swear I'll be single forever."

"You're not hopeless, but you just need to believe in yourself and realize the right man is out there. You'll find him."

I climb out of bed with a grunt. "I need coffee." I'm wearing little shorts and a tank top.

Sadie jokingly whistles at me and says, "I already made a pot of coffee for you. I'm off to paint. I have to get ready for the art gallery."

"You're awesome. I'll be out in a minute." I walk into the bathroom to brush my teeth and freshen up. When I get to the kitchen, I see it's already one o'clock in the afternoon and sure enough there is half a pot of coffee sitting in the brewer. I pour some and pick up my phone so I can check my messages and my social media sites. There is nothing overly interesting online and I'm slightly disappointed when I see there is nothing from Logan. I wonder if he's still in bed. We both work such crazy hours and are total night owls so we would rather sleep all day and be up all night.

"What are you smiling at?"

"Oh nothing." Shit, I was daydreaming about Logan.

"Come on, Sky, it wasn't nothing. You were

glowing and had a smile on your face that reached your freaking ears."

I laugh. "Okay, I was thinking about Logan and what he wears to sleep." I walk back into the kitchen to make a quick bagel so I can eat something before we go out to dinner in a few hours.

"What are you going to wear tonight?" Sadie shouts from the other room. I take my bagel and coffee and head to her painting room, where I lean against the doorframe.

"I have no idea. I need to finish eating and wake up a little bit more before I can think about that."

I watch my friend paint and I have to admit she's pretty amazing. She has painted so many different types of art and I love all of it. Of course, I'm probably partial because she's my best friend, but whatever.

"Are you still going to the gallery showing at the end of the month? I have quite a few pieces that will be out."

"I wouldn't miss it. I already told Dugan's I need that Friday off."

"Great, I could use the support. You know it's a formal event so you'll need a nice dress to wear. This isn't like some of the crappy shows I have been in where you can wear anything you want and be okay. You need to dress really nice."

"I got it, Sadie. I'll make sure I dress nice." I roll my eyes at her concern for my attire and go relax with the rest of my breakfast and coffee.

After finishing, I make one more cup and head into my room to think about my clothes for tonight.

We are only going to Trisha's Diner, but I don't know if he wants to do something else after.

Skyler: Good afternoon, are you awake?

It only takes about a minute before he responds.

Logan: Yes I'm awake. What are you up to?

Skyler: Trying to decide what to wear to dinner tonight. Are we doing something after dinner or do you have to go to work?

Logan: Well if you want to do something after, the club is closed so I don't have to work, but if you don't want to do anything else with me I'll be forced to go to work so I can try and stop thinking about you :-(

Skyler: Blushing…

Logan: I like when you blush

Skyler: Making it worse.

Logan: Dress comfortable Sky.

Skyler: I can't because then I would be going out in these little shorts I wore to bed with this tank top.

Logan: I can't believe you did that to me…I have to go take a cold shower and get ready now.

Skyler: ;-)

That is payback for making me blush. I hate that I blush so easily, but I can't help it. I've always been like this. I choose a pair of gray leggings to wear with a tank top and a long lightweight coral sweater, along with a pair of ballet flats from the bottom of my closet. I head for the shower with my robe and towel.

***

Logan

I have been awake for all of ten minutes when I hear my phone ping that alerts me I have a new message. The club is closed tonight so it can't be anything urgent and I contemplate ignoring it. When I realize it could be Skyler, I grab my phone, curious at what she may have to say.

We go back and forth over dinner tonight. She pretty much told me she's half naked and now I'm picturing her sweet ass body in some little skimpy shorts and a tight tank top. I bet she isn't wearing any panties or a bra and her nipples are probably peeking through her shirt. Now I need to go take a cold shower and relieve this pressure. How the hell am I going to keep my hands off her tonight?

I climb out of bed with my rock hard cock poking up toward my stomach, unable to even piss. I head to the kitchen for some coffee because God knows I'm going to need both strength and caffeine to get through tonight.

I can't believe how late I slept. Despite my late hours I don't usually sleep this late, but my constant thoughts of a certain pretty lady has made it hard to fall asleep. I don't get it because I don't even really know her, but there's something about her. I can't get her out of my head. Every time I close my eyes I picture her sitting at the bar smiling at me. She has the most gorgeous smile, perfect teeth, and those big brown eyes light up her beautiful face.

Coffee mug in hand, I head back to my room so I can figure out what I'm going to wear tonight. Though I want to look good for her, I don't want to overdress. We're going to a diner and I'm thinking about taking her to do something fun. I want to do something where we can laugh and have a good time, and get to know each other too.

I head for the shower, setting the water to slightly warm to help my hard on, and quickly shave before I jump in.

***

Skyler

I'm standing in the mirror checking out my outfit and I realize I'm nervous. I haven't been on a date with anyone since my ex, and that ended about eight months ago. He was a total ass. I swear it took him longer to get ready to go out than any woman I know. He was always late and he couldn't give a girl an orgasm if you gave him step-by-step instructions. Truthfully, I think it was because he cares about himself more than the girl he's with.

"Sadie, do I look okay?" I ask, standing in the doorway of her paint room. She takes a minute to finish what she's doing on her canvas before she looks up.

"You look amazing and you always do. Be yourself and have some fun."

I have thirty minutes before my date and we are about twenty minutes from the diner. I get my purse and keys and head out the door.

I pull up to the diner and head straight in to get us a table. I love this place because everyone in here is so friendly and the food is decent. Also, I love supporting local mom and pop places that have a hard time up against some of the busier, more popular restaurants. This place seems to hold its own. It almost always has a decent crowd of people here.

The waitress comes over, and I tell her I'm waiting for someone else and that he should be here any minute. She drops two menus and tells me she'll be back with some water while I wait. I send Logan a text.

Skyler: I got us a table inside.

Logan: I'm pulling in, sorry, got stuck in traffic.

He walks in, spots me immediately, and heads over. "Sorry I'm late, I was stuck in traffic."

"Technically it's only six now so you got here on

time."

"I know, but I'm usually a few minutes early because I hate being late."

I smile. "Me too."

"Good. We are going to get along well."

He picks up his menu. "Let's order, because I'm starving. Then I can run my plan for after dinner by you."

I glance over the menu even though I know I'm getting the turkey dinner. I love the turkey dinner from here. It comes with the most delicious turkey, stuffing, mashed potatoes, and homemade cranberry sauce.

Logan peeks up from his menu. "Let me guess, you already knew what you wanted."

"I told you, I like this place." I grin.

"Okay then, what's good?"

"Almost anything you get from here is good, but my favorite is the turkey dinner and that's what I'm getting. I also love the meatloaf, or the Reuben if you prefer a sandwich."

"I'll do the meatloaf." He lays his menu down. "So I was thinking after dinner we could maybe go play some miniature golf together."

He's so stinking cute. I'll have to admit to Sadie she was totally right that he wants this to be a date.

"Where's there miniature golf in LA?"

"I know of an indoor place and an outdoor place."

I raise my eyebrows. "Indoor mini golf?"

"Yup, it's really cool. Everything glows in the dark and they use black lights everywhere."

I chuckle. "This I have to see."

32

"Okay, indoor mini golf after dinner it is. Do you want to ride with me and we can leave your car here?" Before I can answer the waitress arrives and asks if we are ready to order. I tell her I want the turkey dinner, Logan orders his meatloaf, and we both ask for Diet Coke.

I look back to him after the waitress leaves. "Where were we?"

"You were about to agree to ride with me to play mini golf."

I burst out laughing. "Oh, is that what I was doing? What if you're some crazy guy who's going to kidnap me, turn dom on me, and then ravage my body?"

"You caught me," Logan laughs. "You're right, you may want to take your car."

Now we are both laughing. "It's fine. I'll ride with you. If Sadie and Jonah like you that's good enough for me."

***

Logan

"I have an idea I want to run by you for the club," I tell her.

"What is it?"

"I'm thinking about giving the club a bit of a classier vibe with a singles night that will have a table with fresh fruit, cheese, and crackers, which will be included in the cover charge, and I've ordered some different wines to start serving at the bar. Patrons will only pay for their drinks like you

33

would at any other club. The part I'm unsure of is the live entertainment. I was thinking of hiring a singer instead of a DJ. Not like a crazy band but someone who can sing soothing, nice music."

"I actually kind of like that idea. Are you going to set a dress code?"

"Yeah, and I already told the staff if they want to work it they will have to dress nicer too. I'm thinking black slacks and button down shirts for the men, but I have to figure out something for the ladies. I'll also list something for the patrons that say no casual attire and list some rules to it."

"I think it sounds like a great idea."

"Would you be more likely to attend on a Wednesday or a Sunday night? I was thinking of doing Wednesday from 7:00-11:00 so it isn't too late, and that will replace my 18+ night now that summer is coming to an end and the younger college crowd will be back to school."

"That's tough. Both nights are work nights, and I can totally understand why you wouldn't do it on a weekend. I would say stick to the Wednesday night. People will like having something to break up the work week and nothing says they have to stay until 11:00 if that's late for them. You can change the hours if you see the place is empty before 11:00."

"Cool. Now I have to start making a promo plan and getting the word out for when the first one will be. The wine I ordered will be in next week, and it's time to line up some entertainment. I'll have to hold some auditions and find a catering company to provide the food so I can figure out the cover charge."

Our food arrives and we start to eat. I'm waiting to see if Skyler will tell me that she sings at local places on the side, though if she doesn't I'll figure out a way to tell her that I'd like to hear her sing for me. Maybe I can find out what night she performs and where from Sadie and pop in to see her.

"You're right, this meatloaf is so good," I say. "How is your turkey?"

"It's perfect. I told you the food here is good. People think small diners like this have crap food but this place is really yummy." She takes one more bite and says, "I'm so full." She pushes her plate away.

"Do you usually eat so little at meals?" I have almost cleared my plate; then again I haven't eaten yet today.

"Actually yeah, and I ate a bagel when I got up. I tend to eat small amounts more times a day, so I'll take this to go and eat it later tonight or I'll have a snack when I get home. I have to keep up my girlish figure, you know."

"Your figure is perfect." The waitress approaches to take her plate so she can wrap it up for her. "I'll take the check when you have a minute too," I say.

The waitress produces the bill from the pocket of her apron and hands it to me.

"What do I owe?" Skyler asks.

"I got it."

"Logan, let me pay for mine."

I shake my head and take a sip of my soda. "Are you trying to wound me? I let you pick the place. I'm paying the bill."

She tries to look mad but fails terribly. "Fine I'll pay for mini golf then."

"We'll see." I laugh. There is no way I'm letting her pay for mini golf either, but I don't want to fight her yet because I don't want her to go home instead of coming out to have fun with me.

When we get to my car, I remember I have the top down. "Do you want me to put the top up?"

Skyler pulls a clip from her purse, gathers her hair up, and grins.

I start the car and drive away.

She's quiet and I'm sure she's thinking about me paying for dinner because technically we said we were going to dinner as friends. However, she has to see I want it to be more than that. I put on some music to try and distract her. She's singing with the music, and she sounds lovely. I can tell she loves to sing. She's glowing and has a huge smile on her face.

The mini golf place is not far from the diner so we are only in the car about twenty minutes. As soon as I park, I jump out of the car and run to her door to open it.

I reach for her hand and pull her toward me with a bit more force than I mean to, and she lands pressed against my chest. She looks up into my eyes with total amusement and I get lost for a moment in her brown eyes. I can smell her sweet coconut scent, and it makes me want to bury my face in her neck to take it all in.

"You know you're beautiful, right?"

Skyler instantly blushes. "I wouldn't say I know I am, but I have been told."

I laugh. "Come on, let's go have some fun."

We walk into the mini golf place holding hands, and once we get inside she's so amused by all the walls painted in black and neon that it gives me the chance to pay without a fight. I hand her a club and a ball and we head off to the first hole. She takes her first shot and gets lucky. Her ball stops right before the hole so she runs up and taps it in so that she gets a two. My first shot I hit too hard and it bounces back at me, so it takes me three to get it in.

"If I find out you're playing badly on purpose I'll be mad at you," Skyler says with her hands across her chest, looking so damn cute.

"Skyler, I promise I did not do that on purpose. I have not played in a long time and I'm not a golfer."

"Well, maybe you should lay off the gym a little. Your big muscles are making you hit the ball too hard."

I bite my tongue because I want to reply 'let's go to my place and I'll show you my big muscle,' but I just grin.

She bends over to pick up the ball and it gives me a perfect view of her ass, and to make it even better, she's wearing leggings. I feel a twitch in my pants and I have to mentally talk myself down. *Down boy, not yet.*

We're about halfway done when her luck runs out and now she's having a hard time. I wrap my arms around her from behind so I'm helping her grip the club. We fit perfectly together and I can't help but wonder if she can feel it too. Not only does she fit perfect against my body, there is a charge

37

between us.

"You're trying too hard. Take a breath and lightly swing the club."

She does as I suggest and gets a hole in one; she's jumping up and down, excited.

"You sure you want to keep helping me? Because I'm pretty sure I'm winning."

I grip her by the waist and pull her against my body, this time on purpose. Her arms go around me and I look into her eyes. "If I get to see that gorgeous smile, I'll absolutely help you."

Skyler bites her lip and bows her head to hide her blush.

We finish our game and sure enough she has beaten me by two strokes. She's ecstatic, making me feel like I'll hear about this again. We head out to my car and before I open the door for her I press her against it. She looks up at me and gives me a flirtatious grin.

"Do you know I have wanted to kiss those luscious lips of yours all night?" She says nothing but smiles wider. I put my thumb under her chin, lifting her face, and pull her lip free with my forefinger before I lower my mouth to hers. I kiss her gently and then hover for a minute, then she lifts her lips to mine. She pokes her tongue out, lightly licking my lips. I open to her and our tongues collide; I hold her by the nape of her neck and deepen the kiss.

After a minute, as much as it kills me, I do the gentlemanly thing and pull away, opening the car door for her. I don't want to press my luck on my first night out with her. She gets in the car looking slightly disappointed, and that's a good thing. It means she's starting to want me as much as I want her. For now I'll take her to her car and let her think about it a bit more.

Chapter 4

Skyler

I can't wait to see Sadie tonight. Our paths have been crossing so we haven't had a chance to talk about my date from the other night. Even I'm calling it a date now. I swear my lips are still tingling from our hot as hell kiss. Logan was so sweet and very much the gentleman. I texted him to tell him I had a great time and thank him for dinner and mini golf, but we haven't talked since and I can't help but wonder if he was disappointed that I wanted to pay for my own meal or if he wanted to do something more and I screwed up somehow.

I'm all dressed up for my gig tonight when Sadie comes walking in the house. "I know you don't have a lot of time, but I want you to tell me all about it."

I laugh at her dramatic entrance. "Hey, Sadie, how's it going? I've missed you around here." She jumps up from the table, gives me a hug, and says in a fake and over the top tone, "Hi, Sky, I've

40

missed you so much. How was your date with Logan?"

I crack up laughing. "Girl, you're such an ass. I'll tell you anyway though. My date with Logan was absolutely incredible. We went to the diner as planned and then he took me to this indoor mini golf place. It was pretty cool. It was all dark with black lights and neon paint. We had so much fun. He was wearing these jeans that I swear were tailor made for his ass, with a fitted V-neck navy blue shirt and boy did he smell so good."

Sadie's laughing at me. "Are you going to wipe the drool from your face before you head out?"

"I will, but only after I tell you about our kiss."

"Shut up! He kissed you?"

I feel like a teenager bragging about how my boyfriend kissed me goodnight, but it *was* a wonderful kiss.

"We were walking back to his car and he followed me to my side to open the door for me. He pinned me against his car and said, 'Do you know I have wanted to kiss those lips all night?' and then he kissed me."

Sadie's squealing like a high schooler, but I frown thinking about the fact he hasn't called me since.

"What is it? Why aren't you excited?"

I look at her and shrug. "He hasn't called or texted since. I sent him a text to thank him and tell him I had a nice time. We had a brief conversation and that was it."

"Interesting. Maybe he's busy with the club. Jonah says he's having an employee problem and he's trying to figure out some new big idea he has."

"I hope so. I know about the big new idea. He asked me about it the other night. He's working on promoting a singles night that can replace the 18+ crowd on Wednesdays. He's assuming now that the college crowd is heading back to school they're not going to come out as much on a Wednesday night so he'll have a 21+ singles night. He wants to charge a cover that will include a fruit, cheese, and cracker table, and then they can buy their drinks."

"That's kind of cool."

"That's what I said. He wants to have live entertainment, like a singer or some sort of soft music going to so people can mingle and talk without having to yell. He has even ordered wine for the bar to give it a classier feel."

"Sounds like he has a great idea. Did you tell him you sing?"

I make a funny face at her. "No, you know how I am. I'm not going to be like, 'Oh I sing, I'll do it for you.' That is a little forward, and you know damn well that isn't me. What if he thinks I'm not good enough for his club?"

"You know you would be fantastic and he would love to have you. I don't know why you don't just mention it to him."

"He said he was going to hold auditions. Maybe I'll go to it and show him what I've got. That way I go through the process like everyone else and he can decide based on my level of talent not the fact that he likes my ass. Now, I love you and would love to talk more, but I have to go. I'll be home late so don't wait up." I gather my stuff and head for the door.

***

Logan

I can't believe I haven't talked to Skyler since the night of our date. I'm trying to take it slow but her not calling me is driving me nuts. Maybe I shouldn't have let her go that easily. We could have gone for drinks or I could have invited her to my place. I don't have a roommate to worry about, but I felt like that would have been a bit forward. I had drinks with my best friend Trevor last night. We don't see each other much anymore and I was bored because I was all caught up at work so I needed something to do. The bastard busted my balls because I was talking about Skyler all night. When I got home I spent the next hour in my in home gym so I could tire myself out.

My email pings, and it's Jonah telling me that Skyler is singing tonight and he provides me with the location. I plan to show up and act like I'm just checking out local entertainment for singles night and that I had no clue she was singing there. She'll probably kill Jonah, Sadie, *and* me if she finds out they helped me. I don't care. I want to see her and I want to hear her sing. She has the sweetest voice; I bet her singing voice is incredible.

I grab my keys and head to the front of the club. Troy is working tonight, and although I still suspect him of stealing I haven't been able to prove it yet. I checked everything over after the weekend; the inventory looked good and there weren't any suspicious bottle breaks to make up for missing alcohol.

"I'm heading out to check out some local entertainment for singles night. I'm not sure if I'll be back or not so make sure everything is locked up solid and call my cell if you need anything."

If Troy plans to steal again, tonight would be the night because I told him to lock up. Tonight is 18+ night so it isn't overly busy and the bar doesn't do huge business because a lot of the crowd is underage. A lot of the 21+ crowd comes around on the weekend when the younger kids aren't here, but we don't do too badly so I won't have a problem bringing it back in May if this singles night doesn't do well. My bouncers have a hard time keeping an eye out for underage drinking so I put extra staff on to ensure that doesn't happen in my club.

I jump in my car and head straight to the club Skyler is working at tonight. It isn't too far away, but as I pull up I wonder how much they are paying her. It's a dump, but she's doing what she enjoys so I can't blame her. The outside is all dingy brick and it looks small. When I walk in, I look around. There are plenty of empty tables, so I choose a small one in a corner, and a minute later the waitress approaches. I ask for a scotch on the rocks and never even look in her direction. The stage is small and there are round tables spread out around the place, with the bar in one corner. All of the tables only seat parties of two or four so it would be hard to hold any sort of big party here. There are not a ton of people here, and I don't exactly fit in. I'm wearing black slacks and a button down shirt, whereas the rest of the crowd is wearing jeans and t-shirts or polos.

Skyler walks out on stage and the music begins. Her first song is from Shania Twain and she does fantastic.

When she's done with her first song she says, "Good evening, ladies and gentlemen. If you have requests please let one of our lovely cocktail waitresses know and I'll do my best to fulfill them." One of the guys screams out a dirty request and she plays it off well. "Sorry, gentlemen, I only take song requests." She winks and then breaks into an Ashanti song and I can't help the smile that spreads across my face.

This woman can not only sing, but she's beautiful and can handle the crowd without upsetting them. I sit and watch as I enjoy my drink, thinking about how I'll get her to sing in my club. That may take some time but I'm confident it will happen.

***

Skyler

It's pretty busy at the club tonight, and I'm a little nervous, though that's nothing unusual for me. I get nervous before every show. I do this all the time and I'll sing almost anything the club asks me to. I've sung country and western, R&B, and so on, and I always have pre-show jitters.

I walk on the stage to start my first song of the

45

night. I scan the room, and who do I see sitting in the back of the room but Logan. Part of me is mad because I didn't even tell him that I sing, let along *where*. My stomach's doing a flip but I can't lose it now; this is one of my better-paying gigs and I need the money. I don't like singing in front of people I know, and that includes hot guys that I like.

I sing the first set of songs in the order they want me to. During the second set, I'll sing any requests. I pretty much provide a list of songs I know, and some of them give me free reign to sing how I want and others want me to sing in a certain order.

I'm finishing the final song of the first half, and everyone is clapping.

"Thank you, everyone. I'm going to take a quick break and I'll be back to sing your requests."

I walk off stage and straight up to Logan's table.

"What are you doing here?" He raises his eyebrows, and I think he's offended.

"I didn't know you sang here. I came in to check out the local entertainment so I could get some ideas for the club and here you are. You never even told me you sang. How come?"

Why *didn't* I tell him? I have yet to land the big gig so maybe I'm not that good, but I can't tell him that.

"Have a seat, Skyler." He gets up and pulls out a chair for me.

"I don't have a lot of time. I have to be back up on stage in about thirty minutes."

"I guess I better make the most of the time I have then. So why didn't you tell me you're a singer when we were talking the other night?"

"I don't know. I hardly know you, and I guess I'm shy about it. Plus I didn't want you to hire me because you like me and then I let you down. I'm not good at promoting myself or talking about it."

"Skyler, you have a lovely voice. Do you realize the gigs you could have if you knew the right people?"

"The manager here says I'm okay and that he books me because I'm pretty and the guys like looking at me. I need the money and I like to sing." I shrug like it's no big deal.

"Skyler, don't you realize he's only saying that because he doesn't want to lose you? He's breaking your confidence so you won't look elsewhere."

I look down at the table because I don't know if he's saying this because he likes me or because he really thinks I'm that good. The waitress brings him another drink and I ask her for some water with lemon.

"What time are you done tonight?"

"Eleven. Why?"

***

Logan

"Can I see you when you get off tonight? I need to run an errand, but I would like to see you after work, even if we just go for a coffee."

She rewards me with a heart-stopping smile. "I'd like that."

We talk for a few more minutes while she drinks her water, and when it's time for her to head back onstage I tell her I'll be back at eleven. I give her a small kiss and I leave to run my errand. Little does she know I'm going to see a friend of mine about getting her out of this dump and into some better gigs. She'll start with working my club on Wednesday nights, and I'm pretty sure I can get her at least one other gig with my buddy.

I get back to the club at about 10:45, and the place is already quiet, so I have no problem getting a table. One of the waitresses comes over but I tell her I'm all set, that I'm waiting for Skyler. She walks off stage right at eleven and collapses into the chair.

I beam at her, pleased with myself. "Are you ready to blow this joint?"

She grins. "Absolutely!"

We walk out hand in hand and are heading to my car when she stops me.

"I need to get my purse from my car."

When she returns, I give her a quick kiss and open the door for her.

"Where are we going?" she asks.

I walk around the other side and climb into the car. "Someplace we can have some coffee and talk."

I pull into the parking lot to a nearby cafe and find a spot to park. Surprisingly, it appears to be busy for the late hour; then again this is LA. I open Skyler's door and we walk in holding hands.

We head straight to the counter and I order my coffee, she orders hers, and I ask if she's hungry. She orders a bagel with cream cheese and I do the same, then we stand off to the side waiting for our food. When our number is called I let go of her hand to get the tray. I spot a table in a quiet corner and head in that direction.

"How would you feel if I told you I could get you a gig in a much bigger and much nicer club?" I ask after we've taken a few bites.

"I would say how and what do I have to do?"

"For starters, I would like you to sing on Wednesday nights at my club. Of course I'll pay you. Second, have you heard of Club Temptation?"

"Who hasn't?"

"Well, I'm good friends with the owner and I told him about you. He wants to hear you sing, and if he likes you then you get rotated into his live shows."

"Are you serious? I'll admit, I'm excited to sing at your club, but what if your friend doesn't like me?"

I get up from my seat and switch sides of the table because I want to be close to her. I sit so close my legs are touching hers, and I take her hand in mine. "I'm going to help you see how awesome you are. He's going to love you."

"Thank you." She blushes.

"You're welcome. Now what does a guy like me have to do to get a girl like you to visit me in the club tonight?"

Skyler giggles. "Ask. I'm off the rest of the night."

"Will you come visit me in the club tonight?"

She looks at her watch. "I don't know...it's getting late and I'm a bit tired."

I look at her, totally confused, and then I chuckle. "You know what I mean. Okay, will you come visit me at the club tomorrow night?"

"Yeah, I'll call a few friends to hang with while you work, and then I'll see you when you get off. My friend Meghan that works with me at Dugan's is off too, so she'll come out with me, and if Jonah is bouncing I'm sure Sadie will come."

"I think tomorrow is his night off, so I'm not sure he'll want to be in the club, but you can ask them. It's up to you. I have another question. How come you haven't called me at all?"

"I could ask you the same thing," she says with one eyebrow raised.

"Let's clear something up right now. I like you, I think you're funny, gorgeous as hell, and I love your voice. I want you to be my girlfriend and my girlfriend only. I tried to give you space to call me, and it didn't work out too well for me, so now I'm going to tell you like it is."

"Okay," is all she says, no argument, no fighting me, simply "okay."

"Well I have to admit that was a bit easier than I thought."

"Logan, I told you I'm not good at this and I may screw up, which is why I hadn't called you. I was too busy trying to figure out why you hadn't called me. I thought I screwed something up the other night and that's why you didn't call. I like you though." Her blush creeps up her face.

"You keep shocking me with this shyness of yours. You looked so strong and confident with your friends, and when you were on stage you were so bold when you handled the men who were flirting with you, yet with me you're shy and

50

timid."

"You're different, Logan. It's easy to be confident when you're around a guy you could care less about, but when you like a guy and he's as confident as you are, it's hard. My past has been filled with crappy relationships, and that wears on a person."

I rub the back of my fingers across her cheek, tucking a piece of hair behind her ear. "How about this? I promise not to let you screw this one up." A small smirk spreads across her cheeks and she nods slightly. It was barely there but I caught it. I move my lips to hers so she knows I'm going to kiss her and she meets me halfway. I kiss her softly and then caress her nose with mine before I kiss her again.

"Will you come to my place tonight? I want to show you where I live and spend the night with you."

She bites her lip and nods. "Let me text Sadie so she doesn't get worried."

I catch her hand and pull her toward the door. "You can text her from the car."

I can't wait to have her in my home.

***

Skyler

We pull up to Logan's building and the valet greets him. When we get out, the valet gets into the car and heads off to park it. I look at him a bit shocked, and Logan shrugs and walks toward the front door.

"Good evening, Mr. Michaels," the doorman says.

Logan smiles at the man and replies, "Good evening. Greg. I would like you to meet my girlfriend Skyler. When she visits, please be sure the valet puts her car in one of my spots and you see that she's let up right away."

Greg extends his hand to me. "It's a pleasure to meet you, Skyler." Then he looks at Logan. "I'll take care of it right away, sir."

We walk to the elevator and take it to the top floor of the huge building. The elevator opens into a stunning foyer with double doors that open into his actual home.

"Feel free to look around," Logan says. "I'm going to get us a glass of wine so we can relax."

When we walk in, the first thing that catches my eye is the beautiful floor-to-ceiling windows on the left that are arched at the top, and in the middle of them is a door that opens to a huge balcony that overlooks LA. I walk through his open living room with its pretty gas fireplace and immaculate hardwood floors to check out the view. As I suspected, it's amazing. He has this cute little patio furniture set that seats four out there too.

I turn around and notice he's standing on the other side of the living room in his large, open kitchen. There is a huge island that has a snack bar on one side and the gas countertop cooktop on the other side. Behind the island are a state of the art stainless steel convection oven and microwave. His kitchen looks like it has never been used.

He walks toward me and hands me a glass of

white wine.

"Your home is lovely. Do you cook?"

He laughs. "Why do you ask?"

"You don't look like one to cook, and your kitchen looks like it has never been used."

He bursts into laughter. "You're half right. I actually do enjoy cooking, but I have a housekeeper who comes in daily to clean and make sure this place stays in mint condition because I'm not home enough and I work too hard to worry about it."

I can't imagine ever being able to afford a housekeeper, so I sip my wine.

"Come on," he says, "let me show you the upstairs and I'll give you a t-shirt of mine so you can get comfortable."

The upstairs is equally as stunning. There is one bedroom downstairs and two more upstairs. One is his and has a master bathroom with a huge tub and shower with his and her showerheads. The walk-in closet is massive, and that is when I see he has way more clothes than me.

He takes a t-shirt from one of the drawers and tosses it to me, but I purposely miss it so it lands on the floor. I decide to mess with him. I have been itching to feel his fingers on me since I met him, and I can tell from the bulge forming in his pants he wants me too. I walk over to the shirt in my three inch heels and bend over to pick it up with my legs spread apart. My dress is so short it gives him a bit of a view. I toss the shirt onto the bed and walk toward him with a look that clearly says *I want you*. He sets his wine glass down on the dresser, then takes mine and sets it next to his.

As soon as his hands are free, he pulls me close and our mouths crash together with wanting and passion. His hands are all over my body and I'm already wet. He pulls away after a minute, panting, his forehead pressed to mine.

"I'm sorry, Skyler. I have no control with you."

I take a steadying breath. "I don't want you to have control with me." I kiss him again, this time a bit slower. When I stop, I look right into his alluring chocolate brown eyes. "Show me how good you can make me feel."

"Are you sure?"

"Logan, I need to know how good we can be together. I can't wait anymore. I've wanted to feel your hands on me from the moment I met you."

He steps away for a minute, running his hands through his hair. "Sky, you don't know what you're saying. I like to play rough sometimes. I like control in the bedroom, and I need you prepared for that."

I know we are going to be good together. I can feel it.

"Show me, Logan. I've never had a sexual relationship that has satisfied me; maybe this is what I need."

He narrows his eyes. "What do you mean?"

"I mean my partners have always cared more about themselves than me. The one partner who came close was a total asshole and treated me like shit so I ditched him. He thought because he was okay in bed he could control me in every aspect of my life. I don't mind you having control in the bedroom, but I need control over my own life."

"Skyler, I would never try to control your life.

Tonight I want to go slow. Is that okay? We can try some rougher stuff another night."

I bite my lip and nod, excited because I thought he was going to say he didn't want to sleep with me. He kisses me gently, pulling away to lift my dress over my head. "You have the sexiest body, Sky." He walks around me, checking out every inch as his hand skims over various parts of me. "Your skin is flawless and you have an amazing ass." He stands behind me and unhooks my bra; it slides off my shoulders and falls to the floor. He grabs the string of my thong and rips it off my body.

I can't help but giggle. "If you do that every time we have sex you're going to owe me some panties."

He leans in and whispers in my ear, "Guess I'll be buying you a lot of panties then." He bites my earlobe and I whimper.

I'm now completely naked and Logan is fully dressed. I start to pull his shirt from his pants while he undoes the buttons on his sleeves and slips it over his head. He has a perfect body. His chest is smooth and well defined just like I pictured. He kisses me again as I lower the zipper and reach in to feel his length, shuddering at how big he is.

He walks me backward until the back of my knees hit the bed, then he pushes me down onto it and finishes removing his shoes and pants. I kick off my heels at the same time.

He climbs on top of me and whispers, "Those heels are hot as hell, and sometime soon I will fuck you in nothing but those shoes."

I turn red, and I know I do because I can feel it. He laughs and kisses me again. His hand is on my breast, kneading and rolling my nipple, and it's setting my skin on fire. His hand glides down my body slowly until he reaches my folds and feels how wet I am for him. He rolls his fingers over my clit and I moan in his mouth.

"You'll always come first in my bed. Do you understand me?" He's playing with my clit and my hips are grinding against his finger. "I'm going to have so much fun teaching you who is in charge. You'll even learn to come when I say you can come."

I moan again. "Logan, I can't do that."

He stops as I'm about to come. "You can and you will. Do you want to come?"

I'm panting. Of course I want to come. What is he thinking? I simply nod.

"Say it. Tell me you want to come."

I close my eyes and take a calming breath. "Logan, I want to come."

He gives me a proud smile. "Good girl." His fingers start to do their magic, and as I am about to explode he rams his fingers deep inside me so I explode around him. "That's it, baby, ride my fingers."

I have no idea how he has so much control over my body already, but that was incredible.

He pulls his fingers from me and brings them to my lips. He glides them over my lips and then licks my lips, tasting me.

"You're delicious," he says. He sticks his fingers in his mouth to lick all of my juices off of them. I can't believe he did that, it was so hot. "I need to be buried deep inside you, so I hope you're ready."

Logan takes a condom from the night table and slips it in place. He positions himself between my legs and slips himself inside of me, closing his eyes to savor the feeling. He's sliding his length in and out of me, but his control is slipping. He picks up the pace and next thing I know he's pounding into me.

I'm meeting him thrust for thrust. "Logan!" I scream as my orgasm is again building.

"Come on, Sky, give it to me. I can't hold out much longer."

My orgasm rips through me and he knows it because he slams into me one more time, and I milk him for every drop. We lay silent for a minute, gaining control over our breathing.

He climbs off of me to get rid of the condom and I instantly feel cold. I snatch up the t-shirt and head to the bathroom as he's coming out. I do my thing and then head right back into the bedroom. He already has the bed turned down so I join him, lying in the empty space he has left for me.

Logan's propped up on his elbow. He looks down at me and says, "I don't know how, but I knew we would be great together."

Chapter 5

Logan

I wake before Sky and despite the fact that I would love to wake her in a much more sexual way, I decide to show her that I do in fact have cooking skills. I head down to the kitchen and start making us some breakfast. While I don't know what she likes, she has mentioned eating healthy, so I make some scrambled eggs with peppers and onions. I cut up a fruit salad and I have some potatoes roasting in the oven. If she doesn't come down soon, I'll have no choice but to put the eggs in the oven with the potatoes to keep them warm and come up with a fun and creative way to wake her.

My dick hardens at my thoughts of waking her with a vibrator to her clit or my teeth clamped down on her perfect little nipples. I shake my head, willing myself to stop or I'm going to end up fucking her over on the couch. I hear footsteps. Thank God she's awake because I was starting to lose it.

"Good morning," she says, looking amazing in my t-shirt and well-fucked hair. She has an elastic in her hand and is pulling her hair back as she approaches. When she lifts her arms to tie the elastic her shirt lifts up, almost revealing what's underneath. I happen to know she isn't wearing anything because I tore her panties off last night.

"Be careful," I growl, "or we're not going to get to breakfast." I reach for her and pull her to me. She wraps her arms around my waist, hugging me as I go for a kiss.

She pulls away and pouts. "But it smells so good and I'm starving."

"Fine. Food then sex."

Skyler laughs. "What can I do to help?"

"Actually, I have everything ready. All you need to do is make yourself a cup of coffee. The cups are right there," I say, pointing to the cabinet where my coffee cups are.

She reaches up and gets two, one for her and one for me, and because she has to stretch I get a glimpse of her naked ass.

"Okay, no more reaching for you. Please make your coffee and have a seat before I take you over my counter." She looks at me in total shock. "Yes, Sky, that's what you do to me. Look." I show her my hard on that's trying to break through my lounge pants.

"Would you like me to take care of that for you?" She grips my cock and squeezes it.

"Woman, do not push me. I want to feed you first." She gives me the cutest pout, lets go, and walks over to the stool with her coffee.

I serve her a plate of eggs, potatoes, and fresh fruit.

"Logan, this all looks so good." She waits for me to sit before she starts eating, and it makes me smile.

"Did you text your friends about going to the club tonight?" I ask. "I'm going to reserve you guys a VIP section so you don't have to worry about seats and you can come and go from there as you please."

She swallows her eggs. "No, I totally forgot, but I can text them right now. You don't have to give us a VIP section though. It's no big deal."

"Skyler, you're my girlfriend and I'm the owner of the club. There's not a chance in hell you will not have a VIP section and you will not pay to drink in my club." She gives me a look like she wants to say something. "Listen, I told you I wouldn't take over your life and I won't, but do not argue this with me."

She kisses me and says, "Thank you!"

I nod. "That's much better. You're welcome."

Skyler takes her phone from her purse that she left on the couch last night and sends a group text.

Skyler: We have a VIP section at Club Thrive tonight who's in?

"All sent," she says.

She gets a response back and tells me it's Sadie and that they are in. She texts back and forth in between bites of her food.

She bursts out laughing, and when I ask her what

is so funny, she shows me the text she got from her friend Meghan.

Meghan: I'm in but hold up, how did you get VIP.

"Tell her," I say.

Skyler: I'm dating the owner.

Her friend texts her right back.

Meghan: Shut the fuck up!

Skyler cracks up laughing again and shows me the message.

I laugh along with her. "You girls are crazy!"

She looks at me dead serious with her eyebrow raised. "You have no idea. Are you sure you can hang?"

"Is that a challenge?" I say, looking at her with the same dead serious look.

"You better believe it. I'm liking you more and more every day, and I need to know you're real."

"Oh I'm real, and you better believe I'm up for a challenge."

She goes back to texting her friend back.

Skyler: I will not shut the fuck up. I'm at his house right now and showed him your text.

Meghan: lol see you tonight girl.

She tells me she's waiting to hear from Rick and Shelly and her friend Katie. She's hoping to hook Katie up like Sadie did us because she needs to find a boyfriend and soon. "I think Shane is single," I say.

"The guy you were working the bar with?" I nod and she takes the last bite of her breakfast. "He's kind of cute. I think she'll like him." Her phone pings and she tells me Katie's in.

"Hey, don't be checking out my bartenders. I can be a jealous and protective guy and you, pretty lady, are mine."

She rolls her eyes at me. "Logan, I didn't mean it like that. I meant that he's attractive and would work for her. Didn't you notice my eyes were only on you the first night we met?"

"No, I was too busy working and watching you shake that ass of yours."

"Then you should have noticed I wouldn't dance with anyone. I don't play petty 'make my boyfriend jealous' games. I don't have time for that, and to be honest, I have messed up enough relationships. I don't need to add to it."

"Why do you feel like you have screwed up so many relationships?"

"Even before I moved to LA I would have crappy relationships. If the guy was nice then he sucked in bed. I wasn't mean enough to be like 'hey our chemistry sucks or you didn't really give me an orgasm last night so I'm going to have to break it off with you,' so I would do stupid shit and sabotage the relationship. I guess I'm not good at communicating. I finally had a great relationship with a great guy and I screwed it up. I told him I was going out with my girls one night and that we were going to one club, we ended up at another, and he was there, but I didn't know. I was dancing and some guy came up behind me and started dancing with me. When the dance was over I told him I had a man and walked away but my boyfriend saw me dance with the guy and got pissed. When we got home he hit me, so I told him I was done. I left and never saw him again."

She won't even look at me, and it's probably because I'm so pissed. I want to track this guy down and punch in him the throat.

"Skyler, if you're worried I'm going to be pissed, I'm not. I know I said I can be jealous but I would never hit you. I may ask you not to dance with other guys, and it may piss me off to see a guy creep up on my lady, but I won't hit you over it."

"You look so mad," she says, looking like she's fighting back tears.

"I am, but not at you. I don't care if you banged the guy in the back alley. No man should put his hands on a woman like that. When I talk about playing rough with you in bed it's different. It's sexual and consensual. If you try it and you don't like it then it stops, end of discussion."

She shows me her gorgeous smile and nods. "I don't mind trying it," she says in a flirty tone.

"Come on, let's go shower." I hop off my stool to put my plate in the sink. "Will you stay with me again tonight since you're coming to the club?"

"Sure, but I have to work Friday and Saturday night, so I'll have to go home tomorrow to get ready and won't be able to stay the night."

"Okay, we'll have to work out our schedules so we can make sure to make time for each other. Want to do dinner again on Monday? It seems to be an easy night for both of us and it will give us a routine."

"Sure. What about this mess?" She adds her dish to mine in the sink.

"My housekeeper will take care of it. I also have to warn her that you'll be around so you don't scare her. She should be here in a little while. I'll introduce you."

"I need a ride to my car so I can get some clothes from home to go out tonight and to wear home tomorrow."

She follows me upstairs to shower.

***

Skyler

I pick up my dress and bra from the floor and place them on the chair. When I reach for my ripped panties Logan laughs.

"I enjoyed doing that."

I roll my eyes. "I'm sure you did, but don't be mad when I show up with no panties on because you have ripped all my thongs and there is no room in my budget for me to replace them."

He shrugs and turns on the water in the shower. "That's one less thing to get in the way of that sweet pussy of yours."

I step into the shower and notice he's semi-hard

again. I glide my hands slowly over my body while the water rains down on me. I close my eyes and tip my head back to wet my hair, and when I open them Logan's standing in front of me fully hard.

"Do you have any idea how much I love that I make you that hard?" I tease.

"I can tell. That was quite the show."

I rub my hands down his chest, grab his rock hard cock, and lean up on my tiptoes to whisper in his ear, "It ain't over yet." I bite his earlobe and his cock twitches in my hand. I run the tip of my tongue down his chest and stomach until I reach the head of his cock. I kneel and suck the head in my mouth briefly before I remove it and lick it shaft to tip. I do it again, though this time I press harder, and when I get to the tip I take his head in my mouth, rubbing my tongue all over it.

"Holy shit, Sky."

I start sucking him deeper and deeper until he's hitting the back of my throat. Logan's thrusting his hips so he's fucking my mouth and I love it. He's hitting the back of my throat and I keep taking him as deep as I can. I glance up to see him looking down at me in shock, and it only makes me want to work him more. I take his balls in my hand and start massaging him.

"Skyler, I'm going to come. If you don't want me to come in your mouth then you need to stop now."

I keep going until he explodes in my mouth, and I swallow him down until I have every last drop.

I stand up and when I do his mouth meets mine and he pins me to the wall. "My god, woman, that was fucking amazing."

I smile at him, proud of myself.

"I hope you're not sore from last night because I want to take you right here in my shower." He kisses me again, then stops to take my nipple in his mouth, and I moan as he sucks one and massages the other. I can feel his erection growing between us and I can't believe he's already hard again. His fingers separate my folds and slip inside of me, sliding them in and out of me and it makes me want him more.

"Please, Logan, give it to me."

He continues to tease me with his fingers as he's kissing my neck. "I promised to never hurt you," he says between kisses. "So be patient."

"Logan, you're not going to hurt me. Please, you're killing me."

He removes his finger and lifts me up with my back pressed against the shower wall and my legs around his waist. He slides himself inside me and I groan.

"Fuck, a condom," he says.

"I'm on the pill and clean, I promise," I say quickly, not wanting him to stop.

"I'm clean too. I have never gone without a condom." His head is buried in my neck and he's balls deep in me but not moving. "You feel so fucking good." The thrust from his hips is pressing me into the wall. "I can't stop now."

I use the wall to force myself against him. His hips are drilling in and out of me and my orgasm is already built up from him finger fucking me.

"Give me what I want, Sky."

I grind my hips with him, bite his shoulder, and scream. My orgasm is tearing me apart. He groans, and I'm pretty sure it's because I'm milking his cock for every last drop, not because I have left marks on his shoulder.

He lifts me so he can pull out of me and slides me down so my feet are on the floor, but my legs are weak so he helps hold me up. He rests his forehead to mine. "I'm sorry. I've never done that before."

"It's okay. I promise I'm on birth control, and like you, I've always used other protection so we're good."

He takes the soap and rubs it between his hands to wash my body. "That was amazing, but I can't believe you bit me."

I start laughing. "I'm so sorry, I don't know what came over me. I've never bitten anyone before. Then again, I have never had sex like ours either."

"So you're not going to do something stupid because our sex sucks?"

I laugh at his joke. "No, it definitely doesn't suck." I rinse off and he washes himself.

When we get out of the shower his phone is ringing.

"Hey, Troy, what's up?" he answers.

Logan becomes aggravated, running his fingers through his hair and pacing the room.

"Are you shitting me? Troy, I left you in charge for one night." He grins then and I'm confused. He's nodding now, not saying anything. "Fine, I'll deal with Shane tonight."

"Is everything okay?" I ask when he hangs up

the phone.

"It's fine, sorry if I scared you. That was a show. I think Troy is stealing from me. He called to tell me I need to talk to Shane because he broke two bottles of alcohol last night. I know Shane well enough to know he didn't do that. Troy is covering his ass, and now I have to figure out how to prove it."

I slip my bra and dress back on while he's telling me all of this.

"Skyler, I need to take you to your car and then get to the club so I can view the footage and see if there's anything suspicious. Then I have to call Shane so I can talk to him before he gets in tonight. He's my head bartender and he's good. I need to make sure I don't lose him because of this."

"That's fine. I'll head home, pack a bag, and relax a bit before we head out tonight."

"When you get there, tell the doorman you're my girlfriend and he'll make sure you're escorted to your section and they'll let me know that you have arrived. I'll come see you first chance I get. It's only a Thursday night so it shouldn't be too busy."

"No problem, I'll be there when you're done. If it's okay, I'm going to try to get a ride with Sadie since I'm coming home with you, if you don't mind taking me home tomorrow."

He kisses me. "That sounds like a perfect plan."

***

Logan

I just dropped Skyler off and I already miss her, but I don't have time to think about it right now. I need to get to the club before anyone else does and look over the inventory and the videos from last night. While I'm driving there I call Jonah on speaker phone.

He answers immediately. "Hey, Logan."

"Hey. Heard you're coming to the club tonight. What's the matter, can't get enough?"

"Nah, my girlfriend misses her best friend," he laughs, "plus I figured it would give me a chance to keep an eye on things on the down low."

"You're the man. That's exactly why I was calling you."

"Did Troy call you about last night?"

"Yeah, how did you know?"

"Because he was being a prick all night. Shane was busting his ass as always. I think he left once to take a bathroom break, and when he finally went to the back to get some bottles he found his name was on the sheet with two bottles broken. He said it isn't even his writing. Then Troy told him he was going to talk to you about him being so clumsy."

"How do you know all of this since you don't have keys to the back?"

"Because Troy and Shane almost threw down on the floor, I had to separate them, and I took Shane outside to calm down because he was pissed. He said he was going to lose his job because Troy had it out for him and he told me what happened."

"Okay, thanks for the heads up. It's time I hide a

camera in the liquor closet, but that stays between you and me. No one else can know or word will get out. I want to catch that motherfucker red handed."

"You got it. Shane is waiting for your call. He thinks he's being fired today."

"He's my next call. Troy is an idiot if he thinks I'm firing my best bartender. I'll see you tonight."

I pull up to the club as I'm finishing my conversation with Jonah and I see Troy is already here. What the hell is he doing here already?

I text Shane.

Logan: I'm going to call you in a minute from my cell when I walk into the club and I'm going to yell at you. I'm putting on a show for you know who, but it isn't real and you're not being fired, am I clear?

I wait for a response and it literally takes a second.

Shane: I got it.

I get out of my car and dial his number as I head into the club. Sure enough, there's Troy behind the bar counting bottles.

"What the fuck, Shane? You have to stop breaking shit. This is costing me money!"

I pause for a minute and Shane says, "Dude…"

"Don't give me any lip about it. The next bottle you break comes out of your paycheck, and if your clumsy ass keeps this up I'm going to fire you." Now I'm in my soundproof office with the door shut and locked. "Sorry, Shane, that was for show because I'm trying to figure out why Troy is in my club already. He called me earlier to tell me you broke bottles but I knew he was full of it, and when I saw his car here I wanted to boost his ego by yelling at you."

"Did you talk to Jonah?"

"Yeah, he told me how you had only gone to the back for liquor once but your name was already on the sheet for two broken bottles. Why you getting so clumsy on me?" I tease.

"Dude, that's not even funny. I wanted to punch Troy in the face."

"Don't do that, then he'll call the cops, you'll get arrested, and I'll have to bail you out on the down low and suspend you until I prove it's Troy."

"You do think it's him stealing?"

"I *know* it's him stealing and I have a plan. Please bear with me, okay? I'll try to put you guys on opposite shifts or something for now."

"Thanks, Logan."

"Alright, I'll see you tonight."

"Later."

I walk out of my office and head straight to Troy. "What are you doing here so early?"

"I figured after I saw Shane's name on the list with the two broken bottles I would check the bar counts to inventory."

"How many times do I have to tell you that is my problem not yours? I'm not paying you to be here. You do realize that right?"

"I know, I want to help you out."

"Well, thanks for the help, but I got this. You

71

can head home and I'll see you for your shift tonight."

He storms out of my club and slams the door, pissed off that I won't let him 'help' me figure out what's going on. I wanted to ask him if the bottles broke what was there to figure out, but I don't want him to realize that I'm on to him either.

I head back to my office to make a call to the company who installed my cameras and ask them when they can do an emergency wireless install. Luckily, they can get out here this afternoon before 5:00. After making the arrangements, I sit down in front of the screens to review the footage from last night. As I suspect, I find nothing that proves Troy took the alcohol so I'll have to wait until the camera is up to catch him. I text Jonah to fill him in.

Logan: I have a plan. Are you ready to bust him Saturday night?

Jonah: For sure!

Logan: If we don't catch him tonight we will Saturday night. Come to my office when you get here and I'll fill you in.

Jonah: Will do.

***

Skyler

I'm wearing a cute top with a pair of navy blue

leggings and calf-high boots. I have my bag ready to go with extra panties just in case Logan rips another pair, and two outfits for tomorrow. We're waiting for Jonah to show up, and Sadie is pacing.

"Where the hell is he?"

She's totally frustrated and I don't know why. It's plenty early and we have a reserved section, so it's not like we have to worry about seating. He's picking us up and taking us to the club because he and Sadie are coming back here after and I'm going to Logan's house. We hear the horn outside and Sadie rolls her eyes.

"I know parking sucks, but I hate when he toots the horn. Why can't he call me or text me like most people do?"

I shrug. "He's your boyfriend."

We arrive at the club after an intense car ride there. Sadie was so mad at Jonah and I don't know why. I tried to get her to talk to me while she was getting ready, and all she would tell me is he has been acting weird lately. He even tried apologizing for the horn, but she's in a shitty mood and I feel bad for him.

When we get to the club, Jonah knows the guy at the door and he tells him I'm Logan's girlfriend and that Logan has a table for us.

He touches a button on his ear wig and says, "The boss's girl is here. Who's taking her to her table?"

A woman appears and introduces herself as Kelly. So this is Kelly. She's the reason I met Logan in the first place since he was working her place as bartender the night I came in and she was out sick. I'm tempted to thank her but I don't want to upset Logan so I keep it to myself. She takes us to a great corner section that we have all to ourselves, right by the dance floor. Kelly tells us she's our waitress, and we give her our first drink order. When she comes back with it she lets us know that she'll be around to check on us. We enjoy our drinks while waiting for the rest of our friends to show up, and sure enough as we are finishing round one Katie and Megan arrive, and as usual Rick and Shelly show up late.

After Kelly takes the drink order, everyone gets comfortable. Jonah says he'll be back, that he has to go see Logan for a minute. We start talking and catching up. I tell them how Logan came to hear me sing last night and he wants me to sing for his singles night here at his club.

"Singles night?" Katie remarks. "Sweet, I need that. B.O.B and I are not on speaking terms right now and I need to take the edge off." We all burst out laughing because it's totally like Katie to throw out there that she's not getting sex.

"Wait," I say, "who the hell breaks up with their sex toy?"

"Me, when the batteries run out," she says.

We all erupt into a fit of laughter again, and poor Katie sits there pouting.

I scan the bar for Shane, trying to figure out how to introduce him and Kelly. Maybe I can at the end of the night if I can get her to stay that late.

An arm slides around me, and I look up to see Logan at my side. I smile and give my man a kiss.

"Hey, sweetie, what are you thinking about? You

were in a daze."

"I was trying to figure out how to introduce Katie to Shane," I whisper in his ear.

He laughs. "Good, 'cause Shane can use a distraction right now."

Megan shouts, "You going to introduce us!"

"Sorry, everyone this is my boyfriend Logan, owner of this fine establishment. Logan, this is Katie, Megan, Shelly and Ricky. Of course you know Sadie and Jonah, or I wouldn't know you."

He says hello to everyone then he tells me he has to go back to work but he'll swing back over when he can. He gives me a pretty steamy kiss and tells me to have fun with my friends.

"Later," I say. When he walks away I look back and their chins are dropped.

"You two are hot together!" Megan shouts.

"Shut up, let's go dance!" I stand, ready to hit the dance floor. The girls follow me, and Jonah and Ricky stay back to hang out and watch us dance.

We head straight for the dance floor and start dancing in our own little circle. The area Logan set us up in has a bouncer right in the corner and I can't help but think he stuck us here on purpose. The bouncer was probably told to watch us and make sure no one bothers us. I'm not sure how I feel about this. On one hand it's sweet that he's looking out for us, and on the other hand I have to wonder if he doesn't trust me after our conversation today and that kind of bothers me. I'm going to ask him about it tonight when we get to his house.

We get back to our section after dancing a while and find Jonah and Ricky deep in conversation. We are tired and sweaty. We flag Kelly down and she brings us another round of drinks. We all sit down and relax for a few and then I notice Jonah is on one knee in front of Sadie with a box in his hand.

"I know I screwed up today and you're mad at me, but please know it was because I was nervous. Sadie, I love you with all my heart and hope you can forgive me. I want to spend my life with you. Will you marry me?" My friend is now crying and nods. Jonah slips the ring on her finger and they stand up and embrace each other.

Logan comes over with a tray of glasses, and he tells Jonah congrats and that the champagne is on him.

I'm not too happy with him right now, but this makes me ease up a bit. I'll be bringing this up later; I don't want to ruin my friend's engagement.

He sits next to me and asks, "What's wrong?"

"Nothing. I don't want to talk about it while our friends are celebrating."

"Promise we'll talk later?" he asks and I nod.

***

Logan

"Are you ready to go?" I ask Skyler

I have to admit I'm a bit nervous right now. She seems mad and I have no idea why. While I want to give her a chance to bring it up, at the same time it's bothering me. She was fine until I came over with the champagne. I wonder if she's disappointed that I was really busy all night and didn't have the chance to hang with her more.

Skyler managed to get Katie to stay so she could introduce her to Shane and they seem to be hitting it off, but I want to get out of here. I kick everyone out of the bar so I can lock up.

When we get to my car I open the door for her so she can get in, then walk around to the driver's side to get in myself.

"Thanks for the VIP section tonight," she says, looking out the window. "We had a lot of fun."

"You're welcome, Skyler. You can have that section anytime you want. Just let me know and it's yours."

She chuckles to herself and continues to look out the window. I let it go until we get to my place because I want to be able to look at her when we have this conversation.

We pull up to the building and she lets herself out as the valet approaches. She heads to the door and the doorman opens it. "Good evening, Miss Skyler," he says.

"Good evening, Greg," she replies.

Greg nods at me. "Mr. Michaels."

I nod back. "Good night, Greg."

I race to the elevator to keep up with Skyler. The elevator arrives, and the tension is so thick I could cut it with a knife. For the life of me I have no idea what the hell I did wrong, but she's cute even when she's pouting and mad. The entire ride to my floor is taken in silence.

As soon as I close my front door behind us, I take her arm. "Can you tell me what has you so upset? Because I'm totally lost right now."

Skyler shakes her head at me. "You have no idea?"

"No. Are you mad because I had to work and couldn't hang with you and your friends?"

"What? No, I'm mad because you had me babysat on the dance floor. I opened up to you today and told you the mistakes I've made, and instead of talking to me about it you put a babysitter on me so I won't dance with anyone."

"Skyler, you're not doing this."

"I'm not doing what?" she yells.

"You're pushing a fight on us. Why? I did not have a babysitter on you. You were in a section of the club where I had a bouncer. He's there to make sure things are safe. That is it."

She sits on the couch and buries her face in her hands.

I sit next to her. "I can understand why your thoughts went there, Skyler, but don't try to break us up before we even have a chance."

"Why would you even want me to stay after this?"

"Sky, we click, don't you see it? Our schedules are similar, we enjoy the same scene, and we have amazing sex. Why would I want to throw that away over a misunderstanding?"

"I'm sorry, Logan. I'll try harder. I told you I'm not good at this."

I rub her back to calm her down. "Let's go to bed. It's late."

Chapter 6

Logan

I'm sitting at my desk working when my phone pings. It's a text from Skyler, and I'm pleasantly surprised. She felt so bad the other night that she's been trying so hard to make it up to me ever since. Though I keep telling her it's fine, she hasn't stopped saying sorry. The text she sent me is a picture of her blowing me a kiss.

Skyler: Have a good night, can't wait to see you tomorrow.

Logan: Don't work too hard. You're going to need your energy for tomorrow.

Skyler: Tell that to my boss at Dugan's. It's a Saturday night it will be packed with guys watching sports to escape their wives.

Logan: Maybe I should hire you to tend bar at

my club.

Skyler: Lol you're funny, you know what I mean.

Logan: Yup, those lonely bastards get to stare at my sexy woman all night and yes I'm jealous. I want to stare at you all night.

Skyler: You can tomorrow night and Monday night.

Logan: and Tuesday night?

Skyler: Lol. we'll see. I got to go, Sadie's here and I need to figure out what we're doing about her apartment. I think she's moving in with Jonah.

Logan: Okay, talk to you later and please think about working for me I'm going to need a new bartender soon.

I want to send Skyler some flowers to work tonight. I pick up the phone and call a local florist and ask if they can get me two dozen red roses delivered to Dugan's this evening. She tells me it will cost extra because she's closing in thirty minutes.

"That's fine, my girl is worth it." I ask her to put a note on a card for me and dictate it to her:

Missing you and your beautiful smile.

Can't wait to see you tomorrow.
xoxo Logan

The florist promises to have a vase of roses delivered by seven-thirty. I smile, hoping this will put an end to the constant apologies and move my thoughts back to work.

I'm thinking about promoting Shane after he has had to endure all of Troy's crap, but first I want to make sure I can nab Troy for the thefts. I have checked the camera several times to make sure it's working and that no one can tell it's there. The staff will start to arrive soon and Troy knows he's a runner tonight, so I'll be spending a lot of my night keeping an eye on these cameras and working on the contracts for singles night.

I found a caterer to do the food portion of the night, and their price is quite reasonable. I want to rotate entertainment for that night so I have hired a DJ to play fun but lighter music.

The club is going to open in about twenty minutes and my staff is busy getting everything ready. The club looks great, the DJ is in his booth, and bouncers are hooking up their ear wigs so they can call for backup if they need it. After walking the floor I call my bartenders over.

"Okay guys. Shane and Kelly are on the main bar and Josh and Kendra are working the second bar with Troy as a runner." I let them know that I'm impressed with how hard everyone is working and remind them Troy will be available if they need back up at their bar or if they are low on any supplies they are to call him.

Jonah comes over the ear wig to let everyone know there is a line down the block outside and he's ready to open when we are. My team is ready. I tell them to get back to their bars, and I give Jonah the all clear to open the doors. I whistle up to my DJ, give him a thumbs up, and the music kicks on.

In no time my club is filling up and I'm pumped. I love seeing people flow through that door excited to chill with their friends and have a great night. My club is clean and has already built a reputation. I'm strict on my dress code and my bouncers take no crap. I want my club to feel comfortable and be a safe place for people to have a good time. I'm happy with what's going on out on the floor and head back to my office.

When I get to my office I have one ear wig set up on my desk that has everyone's conversations flowing and I have one that I'm talking only with Jonah on. He's now on the floor as a roamer so he can back up any of his bouncers but also meet me at the back room if I need him. I have the camera in there running on one screen and a few other cameras on the others. I purposely picked cameras I thought would catch Troy going from the back room to wherever he's stashing his stolen merchandise.

When Shane requests a bottle of Grey Goose over the ear wig, Troy responds that he's on it and heads to the back. I give Jonah a heads up that he's going to the back room but to stay discreet. I see Troy walk into the back room, he grabs the Grey Goose, signs it out, and returns to the bar with it.

I start working on some promotional signs for

singles night because I want to get them to the printer so we can run live with it the week after school starts. I'm promoting it with a variety of entertainment, but some signs will have Sky's name on it as a live singer. There will be postcards handed out at the door in two weeks as people are leaving and a huge sign will be in the window outside the club. Additionally, I'm running a radio ad on the popular radio stations around here. I have learned promotions are the most important part of this business.

"Logan, you there?" Jonah asks in my ear.

"Yeah, what's up?"

"Did you hear anyone call for liquor on your other radio?"

"No, nobody has called for liquor."

"Troy is heading to the back."

"Okay, hang tight a second."

I watch the camera and I see Troy appear. He takes two bottles, writes something in the log book, and heads back out. "He's leaving. Which way is he going?"

"He's heading to the second bar but walked past it to the employee area."

"Okay, follow him at a distance. I want to know where the fuck he's stashing it."

"I'm right behind him."

"I'm heading to the back. I want to see what he wrote."

I walk out to the floor in almost a jog. I go to bar two first. "Do you guys need anything?" Both bartenders shake their heads and I continue on to bar one. "Shane! Are you guys all set?" He nods and I head to the back. I unlock the door and sure enough there are two bottles signed out as broken. This guy is a fucking idiot if he didn't think I would catch on. I press the button on my ear wig. "Jonah, where are you?"

"I'm watching Troy. He's drinking in the employee area straight from the bottle. He stashed the other one in his locker. I even recorded it with my phone."

"I'm on my way. He's out of here."

I run to the back, and sure as shit Troy is sitting on the floor drinking vodka straight from the bottle. "Those are 'broken.' Are you sure you should be drinking from them?" I say, scaring the shit out of him.

"I can explain," Troy says, standing up hastily. "It wasn't me the other times. I needed a pick me up tonight."

"A pick me up? You stole from me. If you needed a pick me up, you should have bought a drink and brought it to the back, although that would have gotten you fired too because there's no drinking on the clock and you're wasted."

"I swear this is the first time I drank on the clock, Logan."

"I don't care. Every time a bottle is signed out broken it's your writing, and any night you're not here there aren't any broken bottles. I have video of you going into the back room, removing the bottles, signing them out as broken, then sneaking back here to drink them. I've already called the cops and asked them to come to the employee entrance of the club. Consider yourself terminated, and I'll be deducting all the alcohol you stole from your final paycheck."

There is a bang on the back door, and Jonah heads over to open it. Sure enough there are two cops standing there and I know one of them.

"Hey, Mr. Michaels, how's it going?" He shakes my hand.

"Good, John. Listen, I need you guys to take this piece of shit out of my club. He's been stealing from me and he's wasted right now."

John shakes his head at Troy. "Do you have proof?" he asks me.

"I do and I'll be happy to get it for you. Do you want it right now?"

"Nah, I'll come by tomorrow and check out what you have while the bar is closed. He'll be in a cell all weekend anyway so we have until Monday."

"Cool. Here's my card. Give me a shout tomorrow and I'll meet you here whatever time you want, but do me a solid and try to make it after 11:00 please. I'll be here until 2:00am."

"Yeah sure, no problem. See you tomorrow."

The cops leave and I turn to Jonah. "That was awesome! You kicked some serious ass tonight."

"It was your plan, Logan. I just stuck to it. I have the entire thing recorded on my cell."

I shake his hand and nod. "Yeah, well that earned you a promotion to head bouncer. You, my friend, are now in charge of our bouncing crew and will be responsible for hiring your own people."

"Are you serious?"

"Dead serious. It's time I start to build a team that will let me back off a little, and I want you to be a part of it. Don't say anything yet. I'll announce it tonight after closing."

"No problem! Thanks, Logan. I promise I won't let you down."

"Alright, get back to work."

***

Skyler

I walk into Dugan's and I can't stop thinking about Logan's offer to come work for him. While I know I could handle the crowd, and that has always been more of the scene I want to work in, I would have to prove myself so that the others won't think I got the job because I'm dating Logan. Part of me doesn't give a shit because I know I can hold my own. I'm going to sing there periodically anyway so it would be nice to do everything in one club. And I wouldn't have to wear this stupid ass shirt anymore.

I walk behind the bar and talk to Megan about what we need for the night and how it has been so far. She gets here at 6:00, but I don't have to be here until 7:00. She gives me a list of what we need from the back so I head off to get it. I also notice we are low on some of the fruits we need for the bar, so I restock that too. We mainly use lemons and limes because we don't make too many fruity drinks in here, but I get to work on washing them and cutting them so we are set for the night.

A woman appears in front of me with a bouquet of roses, and I look up.

"Excuse me," she says, "I'm looking for Skyler."

86

"I'm Skyler."

"Well, Skyler, you have yourself a very sweet boyfriend. These are for you." I sign for them and pull out the card.

Meghan comes over. "What's it say?"

I show her the card, and she reads it out loud: *'Missing you and your beautiful smile. Can't wait to see you tomorrow. xoxo Logan.'*

"Ooh, somebody has it bad. I mean come on, you just spent Friday night with him, right?"

I nod, smiling ear to ear. "He's so sweet to me and we have so much fun together. I have it pretty bad for him too."

"Hey, Sky, I'm glad your love life is going well and all, but can I get a beer?"

I roll my eyes and head to my end of the bar to get Sammy his beer.

When I return with it, he laughs and says, "Thanks, sweet thang."

I hate that they have nicknamed me that in this bar, and that gives me one more reason to leave. The only person who can give me a pet name is Logan and he calls me by my full name. Funny thing is, I hate my full name coming from anybody else, but for some reason I don't mind when he says it. Actually, I kind of like it.

Thinking of Logan, I send him a quick text.

Skyler: Thank you for the roses. They are beautiful and yes you made me blush when they were delivered. Meg says you got it bad ya know.

I tuck my phone in my back pocket and get back to wiping down the bar. Meg and I try to keep everything as clean as possible as the night goes on so we won't have too much to do at the end of the night. The last thing I want to do at two am is clean a bunch of cups and bar tops. My phone vibrates in my back pocket. I have to ignore it for a moment because a few more guys walked in to watch the game and I want to serve them first. I get them their drinks and set them up on the tab they requested before I check my phone.

> **Logan: I think she's right. Have you thought about what I said earlier?**

> **Skyler: Yes I have and yes I want in. I'm done with this place.**

I put my phone away because if my boss sees me he may send me home. Although I could go work for Logan next week, that isn't how I want to leave. I'm talking with patrons and making drinks, and as the night goes on the place has become standing room only. I have no time to stop or breathe. I tell Meg I'm running to the back for some stuff and that I'll be right back. On my way to the back some drunken guy grabs my ass.

I stop and turn around. "Keep your hands to yourself."

"Oh come on, sweet thang, you have a great ass."

"I don't care how great my ass is. Keep your hands to yourself or I'll break your fingers."

"Aren't you feisty tonight?"

"No, I'm not feisty. I'm also not your grope toy to put your hands on whenever you want. I'm a lady and I damn well deserve to be treated that way."

He's hammered and I can tell he's getting pissed, so I walk away before it gets any further out of control. When I get to the liquor room, I text Logan.

Skyler: Are you serious about giving me a job?

I get an instant response.

Logan: Yes.

Skyler: I'm over this place. These guys are pigs. I'm giving my notice tonight.

Logan: Do you need me to come down there?

Skyler: No it's fine, I'm going to stay behind the bar and have Meg do the chasing the rest of the night.

Logan: Call me if you need me.

Skyler: Will do xoxo.

I get back to the bar and let Meg know I'm done running for the night because if one more guy puts their hands on my ass I'm going to quit and she'll be on her own. She tells me not to sweat it, that she has my back.

The rest of the night went pretty smoothly.

Megan had to do a few runs to the back and things started to quiet down around midnight, so we were able to get almost everything cleaned up. I tell Meg that I have to go see Mitch and I'll be back in a few minutes to help her finish cleaning up.

I knock on my boss's office door.

"Enter!" he shouts, like he always does.

"Hey, Mitch, I need a minute."

"What's up, Sky? I have to finish this report for the owner tomorrow."

"I'm giving you my two weeks' notice."

He looks up. "Are you serious?"

"I am. I have been given an offer to work a bar in a club setting, and I'm going to take it."

"I heard about your rich club boyfriend. Does this have to do with him?"

"Does it matter?"

"I guess not. You'll be missed around here."

"Mitch, the only thing these guys are going to miss is putting their hands on my ass, and I'm tired of it. I'm not some plaything for these guys to get off on. I'll finish the two weeks unless you find a replacement for me sooner. Thanks for the two years here."

I walk out and head back to the bar to let Meg know that I gave my notice and that I'm done in two weeks unless Mitch hires someone sooner. I told her I was going to work the club with Logan. We have everything cleaned up and Meg lets Mitch know we were leaving. I meet her at the back and tell her to go ahead, that I'm hitting the ladies room and then heading home.

"I'll see you next weekend, Meg."

"See ya, Sky. Congrats on the club gig. It'll definitely be better than here."

I walk into the bathroom, do my thing, wash my hands, and step outside. I dial Logan's number and he answers as I'm shoved from behind. I drop my phone and scream.

"What's up, Sky? What, all of a sudden you have a boyfriend and so we have to keep our hands to ourselves?"

"Fuck you!" It's the guy from earlier, and I don't even know this asshole's name. I go to pick up my phone and he shoves me again. "What is your problem? You're drunk. Go home."

He picks me up and slams me against the wall. He grips me by the face. "My problem is you. I see guys grabbing that fine ass of yours all the time, telling you how hot you are, and you flirt with them. Then when I do it you make me look like a fool in front of my boys."

"You *are* a fool!" I scream, trying to get away from him. He backhands me, and the pain brings instant tears to my eyes. I'm a fool. Why did I tell Meg to leave? We both know we should never walk out alone.

He picks me back up again and says, "You're going to learn what happens when you make Billy look like a fool in front of his friends." He hits me again. At this point all I can do is pray that either Logan can hear what's going on or Mitch comes walking out to save me. My face is swelling from his attack. I start to fall forward and he slams me to the wall again, knocking the wind out of me. When I start to cough, he laughs.

91

"Oh I got something you can choke on, you bitch." He lets go of me to undo his pants, and I lift my knee, ramming it into his balls.

"Choke on that, you fucker!" I run to snatch up my phone but I'm not quick enough. He grabs my ankle and I fall to the ground, screaming for help.

A car comes screeching to a halt, two men jump out of it, and Billy goes flying backward.

I'm sitting on the ground crying with one eye swollen shut. I can't see what's going on through my tears. I hear grunting, and then Logan is at my side.

"It's okay, baby, I got you." I hear sirens and can see the blue lights flashing. "She needs an ambulance!" Logan shouts to them.

"There's one on the way," an officer replies. "Should be right behind us."

The officers run over to Billy, who is on the ground pretty messed up. Jonah is standing with Logan. The cop looks at us. "Ma'am, did you do this to him?"

"I rammed my knee into his balls and then couldn't stop kicking," I say through tears. I know it was Jonah who beat him up, but I don't want him getting in trouble after he came to my rescue. "I got away and fell here when I found my phone."

"It's okay, baby," Logan says soothingly. "He can't hurt you anymore."

Chapter 7

Logan

My phone rings and I'm happy to see Skyler's face pop up. I know it's probably cheesy but I made the picture she sent me of her blowing me a kiss her contact picture so I see it every time she calls. I answer the phone, "Hey, Sky!"

She doesn't respond. Something isn't right because I can hear noise in the background.

"Sky!" I yell into the phone, and that's when I hear her scream. It sounds like she's screaming for help. I instantly snatch my keys, race to Jonah, and grab him on the run.

"Jonah, come with me!"

I give the keys to the club to Shane and tell him to lock up once the staff is gone. "I'm coming, baby!" I shout into the phone.

"What's up?" Jonah asks when we arrive at my car. I hand him my phone and tell him to listen. We can hear someone yelling at Skyler. I fly to Dugan's, thankful that my club isn't that far away.

We leave the phone on speaker and Jonah is cracking his knuckles.

"I'm going to fucking kill him," he says.

"Jonah, call 911 from your phone and tell them there is an attack happening behind Dugan's."

He does as I requested and hangs up as we approach the scene. He runs out of the car before I have even come to a complete stop. He's pounding the guy with such anger. I run over and get a few kicks in then I spot Skyler on the ground crying. I run to her and scoop her into my arms. We hear the siren and I look up to see Jonah is by my side. I shout to the cops that we need an ambulance and that's when I realize it's John. He tells me not to worry, an ambulance is on the way.

I have played this scene over in my head all night as I sit here and watch Skyler sleep. I'm sick to my stomach that some fucker put his hands on my girl and over something so stupid as her telling him to keep his hands to himself. At the same time I'm pissed she walked out of that slimy bar alone. She works in a *bar*. How can she not be thinking about her safety? Fuck. How is she so under my skin already?

Sadie knocks on the door lightly and I tell her to come in.

"Sky's sound asleep. The doctor sedated her so she can rest."

A tear runs down Sadie's face at the sight of her best friend lying in a hospital bed.

"She's going to be fine, Sadie. She's bruised up, but as long as she doesn't have a concussion from her head hitting the wall I'll be taking her to my place to recover today."

"How are you?" she asks, sensing my frustration.

"I was scared, and I'm pissed she would walk out of the bar at that time of night by herself. She could have been hurt much worse."

Jonah walks in then, and I say, "Thanks for everything yesterday."

"No problem," he responds. "I got your back." He takes a seat next to me. "Have you gotten any sleep?"

"No. Every time I start to nod off I hear that phone call in my head. The doctor said she should be waking up anytime now."

Jonah nods. "I went back by the club last night to help Shane get everything squared away. He asked me what happened to Troy. I told him he was gone and you would update everyone as soon as you could but not to say anything. I explained that we ran out because Sky was being attacked. He said to tell you he hopes she's okay and not to stress about the club."

"That's cool. I'm offering him Troy's job anyway so no big deal. I need to call a staff meeting to update everyone on what is going on. Sky is supposed to be coming to replace Shane behind the bar but I have to see when she'll be up for it. She gave her two weeks' notice to Dugan's last night, though I'm pretty sure she isn't going to want to go back there now."

"Skyler's pretty strong, Logan. She may want to so she can get over it. See what she says when the time comes."

We talk about the club and other stuff for a bit

longer, and I notice Skyler starting to stir. She's mumbling and thrashing, then her eyes fly open.

Right at her side, I tell her, "You're okay, baby, relax. You're in the hospital and no one is going to hurt you."

She takes a few deep breaths then realizes Sadie is here, and Jonah too. "Hey what are you guys doing here?" she asks.

"Waiting for you to wake up," Sadie replies. "How are you doing?"

"I'm a bit bruised up but I'll be fine." Skyler tries to sound nonchalant but she pretty much fails.

"I called Meg. She's going to visit you later, and she feels bad that she left ahead of you. She says this is her fault and that she should have waited."

"It's not her fault. I told her to go ahead and that I was going to be on the phone with Logan anyway. I wasn't expecting the asshole I chewed out earlier to be waiting for me out back." She looks at me. "Where is he, by the way?"

"I don't know," I reply. "He's here somewhere but they wouldn't tell me for fear I'll kill the bastard for putting his hands on you."

"I thought someone else was going to take care of that last night." She looks at Jonah. "You were a bit crazy."

"I was pissed is what I was. When I saw him on the ground and you trying to crawl away I lost it."

There is a knock on the door. It's a police officer.

"Ma'am, can I ask you a few questions?" Skyler nods, and Sadie and Jonah back up to give him a little room. "Can you tell me what happened last night?"

"I was working the bar. I went to get some beer from the back when the same guy who attacked me grabbed my ass. I spun around and told him to keep his hands to himself. We had some back and forth words and I knew he was trashed so I dropped it and walked away. When we made last call he came up for another drink and I cut him off. I told him he had had enough and asked him if I could get him a cab home. He yelled at me and stumbled out the door." She takes a deep breath and continues with her story, adding in that once he dropped to the ground from her kicking him in the nuts she continued kicking him until she stumbled away to look for her phone.

"You messed him up pretty good," the officer said to her with a hint of pride. "He doesn't remember anything from last night. He had no idea why he woke up handcuffed to a hospital bed. We'll formally charge him with assault as soon as we can get him released from here. Since he can't remember anything, hopefully he'll plead out and that will be the end of it for you."

Skyler thanks the officer and he leaves as the nurse is bringing in her breakfast tray with scrambled eggs, oatmeal, juice, and coffee. She tells us the doctor will be in soon to let us know when Skyler can go home.

Skyler eats, making funny faces.

"What's wrong, sweetie?" I ask.

"This stuff smells and tastes like shit. Please tell me you'll get me something better to eat as soon as we leave here."

I chuckle and kiss the top of her head. "You got it. Anything you want, you name it."

She pushes the tray away. "Anything. I don't care if you cook. I can't eat this."

The doctor walks in as I'm telling her I'll make her something when we get home.

"Ah, the talk of going home. Are you in a hurry to leave us, Miss Jones?" the doctor asks and Skyler nods. He laughs. "Everyone is always in a hurry to leave. It's a good thing for you that you only have a minor concussion, and as long as this good man promises to look after you I can release you within the hour."

"Trust me, doc, she's not leaving my side for a few days. We are both off from now until Wednesday."

"Good to hear. I'll write it up and the nurse will be in with your discharge orders, the most important of which is if you get any headaches or if you feel dizzy you must come right back in, all right?"

We both agree. "Good!" the doctor says, and he leaves the room.

"I'm so glad you're okay," Sadie gushes. "We need to get going, but please listen to Logan and get better, because I'd be really disappointed if I had to ask someone else to be my maid of honor."

Skyler hugs her. "I'd be honored to be your maid of honor."

"No more stupid stunts like this, Skyler. Never leave another club by yourself!" Sadie yells.

"Don't worry, Sadie," I say. "We'll be having a discussion about that when we get home."

"I promise," Skyler says. "I got too comfortable.

It'll never happen again!"

***

Skyler

I'm at Logan's and resting on the couch. He won't let me up to help him with whatever he's making in the kitchen. I'm not sure what it is but it smells heavenly. It's already after lunchtime so I'm starving, and I lay here hoping it's something filling. The doctor said I have to take it easy today and tomorrow, and then Tuesday I can get up and do more things and move around before I have to go to work on Wednesday. I know Logan's worried about me going back to Dugan's, though he hasn't said anything yet. To be honest, I'm not sure I want to go in. I also know he's pissed at me for leaving alone, and I don't know how to bring it up. He showed his dominant side in the hospital and it made me a bit nervous.

Logan comes over with a TV tray and a glass of milk, then heads back to the kitchen to make me a plate. He returns with a grilled ham and cheese sandwich, grapes, and some chicken noodle soup.

"Thank you so much, Logan. I'm starving!"

He shows me his handsome smile. "It's my pleasure, Skyler."

He sits down beside me and I lean on him while I eat. We decide to watch a movie so he goes onto his On Demand and chooses something for us to watch. After I finish eating I can feel my eyes getting heavy, and I doze off.

I awake a short time later to Logan sitting across from me with his laptop on his lap and he looks deep in thought.

"What are you working on, honey?" I ask him.

"You're awake. Are you hungry?" he asks.

"No. I'm still a bit tired. I'm going to rest." He continues typing for a minute then says, "I offered Shane the assistant manager position and he accepted. Now I need to bring you in and get you on the schedule, so I'm working some stuff out as far as who will work when. He covered a lot of shifts as head bartender, but I'm not going to promote a new head bartender right away. I'm going to have Shane manage it."

"That sounds like a good idea. What nights do you want me to work?"

"Friday and Saturday for sure. I'll have you behind the main bar on Friday and the second bar on Saturday. I'm thinking I may make one of the other bartenders a runner on one night and put you on Thursdays as well."

"Okay," is all I manage this time, and I drift off again.

***

Logan

It's so hard to sit here and work while I watch Skyler sleep. I've done more analyzing of how I feel for her than getting work done, but I don't want her to know that because I don't want to scare her. I'm not sure how but this woman has managed to get under my skin and quickly. I've never felt so strongly about a woman in such a short period of time, and it's a bit scary. The anger and rage I felt when I realized she was being attacked is like nothing I have ever felt before. I've never been a huge romantic or believed in love at first sight crap. I've only been seeing her a short time and I know I'm falling for her. Though I'm not convinced she's falling for me. I know she's happy, and I'm confident she cares about me, but is she *falling* for me the way I am her?

I shake my thoughts off and get back to work because I need to work out the new schedule and email everyone to call a meeting announcing the changes at the club. I email everyone and tell them to meet me at the club Tuesday night at 6:30 for a quick meeting, letting them all know that they will be paid for their time. I'll announce that Skyler will be working the bar and singing on the opening night of the singles night. Jonah is now my head bouncer and will be in charge of scheduling, hiring and firing the bouncing staff, and if they have any issues they need to go to him. What I still need to figure out is what I want Shane's responsibilities to be. Troy was only assistant manager because I kept him on from the old club. Now I know why the club was going down the tubes when I took it over.

I work on my laptop for about another hour working out Shane's responsibilities and adding the new singles night to the website of upcoming events. I've ordered the posters for outside and contacted the radio stations I want to promote on. Now I need to put this aside and start making us some dinner.

I head into the kitchen to start getting dinner in the oven. I want to make Skyler something healthy so she can heal quickly and that means protein. I have a pork loin marinating in the fridge, which I pull out and place into a pan. I cut up some potatoes and add them to the pan then head to the fridge for some fresh carrots and snap peas. I peel the carrots and toss them in with the rest of the roast and get it into the oven. It's going to take about an hour for this to cook and while it does, I want to get Skyler to take a bath so we can relax after dinner. I laugh at my desire to take such care of her.

God, I hope I don't end up with a broken heart again.

I head over to the couch to wake Skyler, and she jumps. "Skyler, it's me. You're okay."

She takes a deep breath. "Sorry, you startled me."

"It's okay, I have dinner in the oven. Let's go take a bath so we can relax after dinner."

She stretches and gives me a dirty grin. "That sounds good to me."

"Nice try, but I think we need to refrain from that type of activity for today. I do, however, want to sit with you and wash you."

"And you want me to behave? Do you have any idea how much I love your hands on my body?"

"No, but I'm glad to hear that because after the stunt you pulled leaving the club yesterday I want to put my hands across your ass." I help her off the couch. "Come on, let's go take a bath."

We head upstairs to my huge oval soaking tub. I

walk into the bathroom and start running the water. When I come back out I find her lying on the bed.

"Oh no you don't. No more sleeping for a little while. I want you to have a good night's sleep tonight."

"But I'm tired," she whines. Normally that would piss me off, but she's so cute it makes me laugh.

"I know you are, but come on, we have to get you up and moving." I help her sit up and pull her shirt over her head, then pull her off the bed. I pull her panties down her amazing legs, letting my thumbs skim them the whole way down. She grips my shoulders and steps out of them.

"What, you're not going to rip them off?"

"Not tonight, sweetie," I laugh.

The tub is filled so I shut off the water and help her in before I remove my clothes and climb in with her.

I sit behind her with a washcloth, rubbing the warm water all over her body. I want to talk about how she's feeling about the attack, but I'm not sure if she's ready. I think about it for a minute more, then ask, "How are you feeling?"

She lays her head back on my shoulder. "Tired and a little sore, but nothing too serious."

I kiss the side of her head. "I mean emotionally. How are you doing?"

It's a long time before she responds, and I find myself wishing I had sat across from her so I could see her face.

"I'm okay, I guess," she says after a long moment. "I was really scared because he was trying to get his pants down when I shoved my knee into his balls. I'm pretty sure he was planning to rape me and that scares the shit out of me."

I shift in the tub to look at her. "Skyler, why didn't you tell the cop that? He can up the charges to attempted rape." Her eyes widen from either fear or realization that that was exactly what was happening; he was attempting to rape her.

"I don't know. I was groggy and didn't think about it that way."

"The cop who interviewed you gave me his card before he left. We'll call him later and let him know that you realized there was more to the story."

She nods and closes her eyes, burying her head in my neck.

"What if he comes after me again? Sadie is moving out and I'll be living by myself. I'm scared."

"I'm not going to let that happen and neither will the police. Honestly, I think he was trashed and wouldn't have done it if he were sober."

I'm not sure I believe that, but I know it will calm her down. Being bartenders, we know people do stupid shit when they are drunk.

I squirt some body wash on a washcloth and gently start sliding it over her body, washing her and relaxing her.

"You're going to be okay, Skyler. Please tell me you know I care about you and will not allow anyone to get to you."

She kisses my neck. "I know. I care about you too, Logan, so much it scares me. I have never let anyone become a part of my life the way I am with you. I have never clicked enough with anyone to even try and have a relationship like I want with you."

"I know what you mean. I had one serious relationship not too long before I opened the club and she broke my heart. I think that's why I bought the club. I needed to busy myself. It took me a while to find a place I liked and I spent a good amount of time looking for the perfect spot. I was either coming across buildings that were too beat up and needed a lot of work or clubs that were so far in the red it would take me forever to get them out. It's amazing how many clubs in LA are struggling because of lack of leadership."

"What did you do before you bought the club?"

"I managed another club. Once I realized I was doing all the work and the owner was making all the money, I took the money my mother left me and bought the club."

"I'm sorry. I didn't know you lost your mom."

"Yeah, quite a few years ago. She was big in LA. She starred in a few movies but got wrapped up in drugs and overdosed at a party one night. I'm big on my employees not drinking or using drugs. Anyway, she left me quite a bit of money and I had invested it all and was living off my income from my job. When I bought the club I paid for it in cash so it would be easy equity and I could hopefully be able to get a second one going within two to three years."

"That's pretty cool." Skyler's tone is flat, and I feel like she's thinking about Dugan's and I want to get her mind off it.

"When I saw you walk into the club that first night with Sadie my whole mentality changed. I was in such a bad mood that night. I was pissed Kelly had called out and I was stuck behind the bar even though I knew it was a good place for me to be. I knew it was my chance to earn the respect of my bartenders and show them I can work it too, but I didn't want to be there." I rub her back some more, trickling warm water down it. "When I saw your beautiful face sit down in front of me I couldn't help but smile and I had to fight not to stare at you." I can feel her smile against my chest. "Stop blushing."

Skyler laughs. "How did you know?"

"Because I could feel you smile and I can see it creeping up your chest. You turned my night around. I watched you every chance I could."

"I was trying to watch you too, and I was brushing guys off because I didn't want you to think I was out trolling."

"Let's get out and dry off. The water is starting to chill and I don't want you cold." We climb out of the tub and I wrap her in a big fluffy towel. "Stay here for a minute. I'm going to get you a pair of my sweatpants and a t-shirt. Tomorrow I have some clothes being delivered here for you so you'll have some things here of your own."

She looks at me, slightly angry. "What do you mean 'delivered'?"

"I called a friend of mine who happens to be a personal shopper and ordered you some clothes to be delivered."

Skyler's pacing the room, totally freaking out.

"Cancel it. We can go to my house and get some clothes to bring here."

I run my fingers through my hair. "Why would I cancel it?"

"Why? Because I can't afford a personal shopper. I spent my entire savings getting here and getting settled. I can't go shopping with personal shoppers. You don't understand, when my mom and dad died, I had the bare necessities. Clothes, a bed, and some small pieces of furniture. I had already decided I was heading out west but needed to save some money to get here so I only bought the basics. I even stopped dating because I was too focused on getting here. When my parents died in a car crash they had minimal insurance. I sold everything I could to give them a burial and used what was left from selling everything, including their house, to get here. I met Sadie and have been busting my tail since."

"Skyler, look at me." She stops pacing and looks up at me. "I'm not asking you to pay for this. I bought it because I want you to be able to stay here without having to worry about packing. And, well, because you told me if I was going to keep ripping your panties I would have to replace them."

"You don't understand, Logan. My parents didn't have a lot when I was growing up. I have always had to rely on myself to get what I wanted or needed. They tried hard and loved me dearly but struggled in life."

"Let me take care of you, Skyler. You'll never struggle again, I promise."

"You're asking a lot of me, Logan. I'll try." She

stands tall, slipping on my pants and a t-shirt.

"Good. I know I promised you I wouldn't take full charge of your life, but after this shit of leaving the bar on your own, you're making it hard for me to keep my promise. I want to take care of you. Don't make me take control of you." She nods and then looks down. "Good, now I have to get downstairs before I burn our dinner."

Chapter 8

Skyler

I awake to Logan's arms pulling me closer to him while his legs are intertwined with mine. His hands on me make me want to feel his lips on me too. He hasn't touched me since my attack and I'm aching for it. I want to erase the thoughts of that scumbag's hands on my body. I gently rub up and down his semi-hard erection and I can feel it growing through his pajama pants. He moans in his sleep. I continue stroking him, kissing his chest and licking his nipple. He finally wakes.

"What are you doing, Sky?" His voice is raspy and it sounds sexy as hell.

"I'm trying to wake you in a fun and seductive way."

He laughs and says with his eyes closed, "I don't think I'm ready."

I sit up to look at him. "What do you mean you're not ready?"

"I mean I was really pissed at you the other day

when I found out you left the bar alone and I have wanted to smack that ass until it's beet red ever since. I'm not sure I can control that, and you're not ready for that kind of intensity."

"Who says I'm not ready? Today is Tuesday and the doctor said I could go back to normal activity today if I haven't had any headaches, and I haven't. You don't understand. I have to erase this scene from my head. I need you to touch me so I know we're okay and you still want me after someone else tried to take what's yours."

"You think I haven't had sex with you because another man put his hands on you?"

I nod, no longer able to look at him.

"Sweetie, I never meant to give you that impression. Me not touching you has only to do with you healing, not anything with this asshole hurting you." He rolls onto his side and presses me down into the mattress. He brushes my cheek with the back of his fingers and leans in to kiss me softly on my lips. "You're so beautiful and I want to take away your fears. I'm going to smack that ass of yours, so you'll remember to never leave a bar alone again, and then I'm going to make sweet love to you. You have to promise me if it's too much you'll tell me to stop. I'll try to go easy on you since you have never done anything like this before."

I grin and nod excitedly. He climbs off the bed, pulling the comforter with him. He grabs my legs and pulls me to the foot of the bed, flipping me over so my legs are hanging over the edge of the bed. His bed is so high that my toes barely reach the floor.

He tells me not to move and I hear him moving around the room. I have no idea what he's doing because I'm lying on my stomach, and since I don't want to disappoint him I remain as still as I can. I was already wet for him, and now the anticipation is causing even more moisture to build between my legs. I'm so deep in thought I don't even realize he's behind me until his hand comes down on my ass. I gasp at the sting of the blow.

"Count," he grunts.

I take a deep breath. "One." He bends down and kisses where he hit me then immediately smacks me again in a different spot. "Two." Holy shit that hurts, but it's so hot at the same time. He rubs my ass, his warm hands massaging me gently before his hand comes down again, this time lower, almost smacking my pussy at the same time. I'm lost in the realization that I'm enjoying this.

"Count!" he growls.

"Four."

He laughs at me. "That was three. You earned one more." He smacks me again.

"Four," I say instantly.

"Your ass looks amazing. Two more and I'm going to give you what you want." When he smacks me this time I shout, "Five!" I realize it doesn't hurt so much anymore and now I'm excited with anticipation. He gives me the last one. "Six!"

His hands are rubbing over my ass, then head up my back. His hands are warm, and my skin burns with every touch. He slides two fingers deep inside me and moans in my ear as he bends over me. "Woman, you're so wet from me spanking you. I

111

think you definitely liked that." He continues to fuck me with his fingers. "You did good, sweetie. Now I'm going to reward you with an orgasm, are you ready?"

"Yes please, Logan!" He flips me over and kneels on the floor in front of me. He places one leg over each of his shoulders and buries his face between my legs. He sticks his tongue out and licks up all of my juices like he's licking a popsicle.

He takes my clit in his mouth. "Mmmm," he says with his lips still around my clit, suckling on it, and the vibration nearly makes me combust. He pulls away to start licking it hard and fast. That's my undoing. As I explode his tongue leaves my clit and he buries it deep inside me so he can fuck me with it as I orgasm all over his face.

Once he's satisfied he has gotten every last drop, he stands with my legs in his hands. He slams himself deep inside me and I groan out as I adjust to him. Without pause he's giving me what I wanted. He's pounding in and out of me, giving me every inch of him. His hands are on my hips squeezing them tight, pulling me toward him, forcing me to meet him thrust for thrust. My orgasm is building and quickly.

"Come on, Sky!" He doesn't relent until I give him what he wants. "Yes," he groans as my orgasm tears through me. My legs are shaking. "I love how you milk me for everything I've got," he says as he empties into me.

"Let's take a quick shower and then I'll make us some breakfast."

He pulls out of me, and we both head into the

shower. He seems distant even after we've had incredible sex, and I need to know what's going through his head. I give him a minute to process and see if he'll bring it up himself, but if not I'll talk to him at breakfast.

I start the shower and step in. While I'm wetting my hair, he steps into the shower and pulls me into a hug.

"What is it, Logan?"

He shakes his head. "Wash. I need to feed you."

"Listen, I know you like to be in charge in the bedroom and I'm okay with that, but you need to stop treating me like a kid. I'm your girlfriend."

He looks at me with raised brows. "How am I treating you like a kid?"

"Really, Logan? 'Wash. I need to feed you?' Totally ignoring the fact that something is clearly bothering you. If you're not ready to talk about it fine, say so, but don't act like it isn't there."

He closes his eyes and runs his hands through his hair. I can tell he's thinking about what he's feeling and how to handle it.

After I rinse off, I say, "I'm done here so I'm going to start breakfast. We can talk while we eat."

I get out of the shower, dry off, and head into the bedroom so I can pick something to wear from the clothes he had delivered for me. He made it sound like there were going to be a few outfits delivered. In reality he had an entire wardrobe delivered. It's quite ridiculous.

I head downstairs to make a cup of coffee. I find a box of pancake batter, as well as a pack of bacon and fresh strawberries in the fridge. I start mixing the batter, adding my secret ingredients before he gets downstairs. I turn on the oven and lay out the bacon on a pan so I can get it going before I start making the pancakes. Logan has a griddle built right into his cooktop and it's pretty freaking cool. I love his kitchen and you can tell it's set up for someone who enjoys cooking.

I feel two hands wrap around me from behind. "I'm sorry, Skyler," he says as he kisses the side of my head.

"What are you sorry for?"

He pauses for a moment before he moves my hair to one side and kisses my neck. "I'm sorry for not telling you that this entire event scared the shit out of me. For not letting you know I care about you so much that when I heard you screaming on the phone I was freaking out because I thought I was going to lose you. And most importantly for not telling you...I love you, Skyler. I didn't think it was possible to feel so strongly about someone in such a short period of time, but I do. I have such strong feelings for you that I don't even like what I just did to you. I hate that I spanked you and I wish I could take it back."

I turn around to face him, placing one hand on each side of his face and pull him in to kiss him. "Thank you for being honest with me. I'm sorry I scared you, and I promise I'll never do it again. I work for you now, so I'm sure my new boss will make sure I get home safely." I grin playfully, trying to lighten the mood. "As far as you spanking me, I didn't mind it. If you don't ever do it again because you don't want to, that is okay too, but don't beat yourself up over it."

He smiles and nods at me.

"Good, now let me get to work making you my famous pancakes."

He steps aside. "Famous pancakes, huh? Do you know that I love pancakes?"

"I didn't know that. I hope you like my pancakes." I pour batter onto the now-hot griddle while he makes coffee. The thought is not lost on me that he said he loves me and I didn't say it back. I feel bad that I didn't, but I want to tell him when he'll know I'm saying it because I mean it not simply in response to him saying it.

We sit to eat and he's devouring my pancakes. I wonder if he's hungry from our morning sexcapade or because he's enjoying them.

"What?" he asks when he notices I'm watching him intently.

"Are you that hungry or are you enjoying them that much? You look like you're in college after an all-nighter."

"Both. These pancakes are delicious and that makes me glad that I'm so hungry."

I shake my head and put two more pancakes on his plate, which he quickly devours.

***

Logan

We walk into the club at 5:30. I want to show Skyler around, though first I take her to my office to have her fill out employee paperwork so I can add her to the payroll. I want all of this done before the staff gets here. I need to make sure they do not treat her differently because she's my girlfriend. While she fills everything out, I work at my computer checking on posters and such for the upcoming singles night. We'll be handing out postcards this week to start the promoting and we have flyers up around the club.

When she's finally done I show her which bar is bar one and which is bar two. I fill her in on the rotation of bartending and runners and let her know that tips are shared evenly so runners don't get screwed out of tips for the night.

"I have also come up with a classy vase that you can put on the stage with a rose in it for tips while you're singing. I'll have a few ones in it each night for you at the start of the night so people realize it's for tips. We need to finalize a list of music for that night and have a list of songs patrons can request."

"No problem," Skyler says.

I show her the back room and the sign-out sheet, filling her in on how we caught Troy stealing from me. As we make our way back out to the first bar, Jonah and Shane come walking in.

Jonah gives Skyler a hug. "Hey, Sky, how you feeling?"

"I'm good. Thanks again for coming to my rescue with Logan."

He grins at me. "No need to thank me. That's what friends are for."

"Shane, I'm counting on you to make sure that no one treats Skyler any differently because she's my girlfriend," I say. "When she's here she's part of the team, and I expect her to be treated that way."

"You got it, Logan." He looks at Skyler. "If you have any problems at all, come see me."

She nods at him. "Thanks, Shane."

A short time later the remainder of the team is here, and I get the meeting started. "Thank you all for coming in tonight!" I call loudly to get everyone's attention. "I'm sure most of you noticed that Troy disappeared on Saturday evening, and that's because he has been fired and arrested for theft." I pause. "Yes, ladies and gentlemen, my assistant manager was the one stealing from me. So you all know, I'm pressing charges. I do not take matters like this lightly. I'm telling you because I like the team of people I have working for me. I hope that you like working here too and wouldn't risk your jobs over some alcohol. It doesn't matter who it is. You'll be removed from my club immediately. I have promoted Shane to my new assistant manager, so he won't be working behind the bar with you as much. However, that doesn't mean I'm leaving you shorthanded. Some of you have seen Skyler here around the club already. She's going to be our live entertainment for singles night, and she's also joining our bartending staff as well to replace Shane. I have had the opportunity to see her sing and work a bar, and she does a fine job at both. Please welcome her, because she'll work hard with you. I have one last announcement before I take questions. I have created a new position, head bouncer, and have offered it to Jonah. He has the experience and has been around this club the longest, so if you're a part of the bouncing crew you now report to him, not me. He'll make your schedules and deal with any issues you may have. Please see him going forward. If I need to be involved he'll come to me."

"Now, does anyone have any questions for either me, Shane, or Jonah?"

"Will Jonah still be working the club in the same capacity, or will we be hiring another bouncer to replace him?" one of the bartenders asks.

I look at Jonah and give him the go ahead.

"I plan on still working the club," Jonah replies. "The responsibilities I have taken on as head bouncer will not get in the way of me working the floor, and I still want to be out here with my team."

Most appear happy with his response, though there's one or two who look like they were hoping he would back off, probably so they could get more hours.

"Anyone else?" I ask before I wrap this up.

"What is Shane going to be doing if he won't be working the bar?" Shawna asks.

"We haven't fully ironed out all of his responsibilities yet," I answer, "but he'll be running for you guys, and he's going to be in charge of all bartenders the same way Jonah is for bouncers. If you have a problem or you need time off, you need to go to him." When no more questions are forthcoming, I say, "Are we good?"

Everyone nods and looks pretty happy.

"Good. Then get out of here so I can take my girl to dinner."

When they start filing out of the room, some are welcoming Skyler to the team as they say goodbye, and some leave without saying a word.

I can now take Skyler to dinner and then we need to pick up her car so she can move it to my house for work tomorrow.

We pull up to the restaurant and I walk in, giving my name to the hostess. I eat here often and they know I have a specific table that I like, and we are walked right over to it. I pull out the chair for Skyler and she takes a seat. As I take my seat, the hostess hands us menus and lets us know our server will be with us in a moment.

Skyler's looking over her menu and I'm watching her. The light from the window is reflecting off her beautiful face, and in this moment she looks like an angel.

"What do you want to eat?"

"I have no idea what I feel like eating." She goes back to skimming the menu. "I'm going to have the Asian chicken salad. I have been on carb overload, and if I don't watch it I'm going to look like a blimp on stage for opening night."

"Skyler, you have an incredible body. And besides, I have a gym in my home and you can feel free to use anytime you want."

"Thanks, I haven't been going since you and I started seeing each other and I need to get back to it."

The server arrives and we place our orders for both our drinks and our food. She walks away, promising to be right back with our drinks.

Skyler is staring out the window into the busy evening night. "What are you thinking about?" I ask her.

"A lot of things," she replies, still looking out the window, "like how much my life has changed in the last few weeks. I can say I have never been happier than I am now. I feel like my life is finally moving in a positive direction."

"Why do you feel your life wasn't in a positive direction before? You got yourself here and without the help of any friends or family. I think that is pretty positive."

Though our conversation is a bit heavier than I wanted to have tonight, at the same time, I'm glad we are talking.

"Yeah, but I was lonely before. Meeting Sadie was great and we hit it off right away. But there were many nights she would be with Jonah, and I can't fault her for that. I couldn't handle another crappy relationship or another guy who wanted me only for my body or sex. I needed to stay focused on my goals."

"What about us? Do I fit into your goals?" While I hate that I sound nervous, I'm starting to wonder if she didn't tell me she loved me because she wasn't planning on sticking around.

"You do now. I didn't want to go out the night I met you. I fought Sadie on it, giving her several lame excuses. She told me I was going out and that was it. Now I'm glad I did. I finally feel like it may be possible to sing and have a relationship. I think I want to go in a different direction now." She looks outside again. "Before, I wanted to be famous. Recognition, record deals, the whole nine yards. Now I want to be here and sing at better clubs locally, become known as the local singer to see."

"What has changed?" I ask, hoping it has to do with me.

"I met you. I know you probably think I don't have feelings for you because I didn't say I love you in return when you said it earlier. To be honest, I wanted you to know I was saying it because I meant it not because you said it."

The waitress arrives with our meals, and we start eating.

"Mmm, this is so good." Skyler closes her eyes, savoring her chicken. We both settle into a comfortable silence while we eat, and I'm feeling better about our situation. I want to ask her to move in with me. I'm not sure if she'll be up for that since we are still new. I have to wait to see how things play out.

"Oh, I meant to ask you. Sadie has her art show on Friday. I know that's a busy night in the club, but is there any chance you can escape for a few hours to go with me? Then we can hang at the club after if you want?"

"What time does the show start?" I say between bites. I'm suddenly starving and my food is delicious.

"It goes from 7:30 to 11:00. We don't need to be there the entire time. I promised her I would go and support her because this is her first time in a larger art show. I have to find a dress to wear as well."

"I should be able to make that happen. Maybe I can have Shane open the club and we can go from open to maybe 9:00, and then hit the club since it won't be busy yet. We open at 9:00 but things don't pick up on a Friday night until 10:30-11:00, so that should be fine."

"Great. I'll look for a dress this week. I assume you have a suit you can wear."

"Of course I do. If you want I can have the personal shopper deliver some dresses for you to try on. I'll leave it up to you."

I can see her thinking about it, and secretly I hope she accepts because I enjoy taking care of her.

"That would be nice, thank you."

"Is there a certain color you would like?" I ask.

She chews the inside of her lip for a moment. "Maybe black."

"I'll have her deliver a few different colors and you can keep what you like and what you don't we can send back, okay?"

Skyler smiles and nods at me.

We are on our way to pick up her car and since she hasn't mentioned work tomorrow I ask, "Have you decided what you're doing about work tomorrow?"

"Part of me wants to call Mitch and tell him I'm never coming back. I haven't even told him what happened though, so I feel like that is unfair. I don't know what to do."

"Skyler, when you were in the hospital I called the bar and told Mitch you were attacked outside the club. He knows what happened and didn't give a shit. Personally, I would prefer you didn't go back there. I'll take care of you."

"Is that what you would like me to do?" she asks, and I glance over at her quickly before I look back to the road.

"I want you to move in with me and not worry

about it until you start working the club. I also want you to be happy with the decision."

She's chewing her lip again. I have noticed she does that when she's nervous or thinking about something. "Can I sleep on it?"

"Of course you can. Like I told you before, I want you to be happy and I want to take care of you, but I don't want to rule you. It's your decision. I would be less worried about you if you were living with me though."

I pull up to her apartment.

She leans over to kiss me and says, "I'll see you at your place."

Chapter 9

Skyler

I have three dresses to choose from tonight and I don't know whether I want to wear the black, the blue, or the red one. They are all very pretty and fit me well. I can chose from any of them because Logan is wearing a black suit. I'm leaning toward red or blue. I hold the red one up one more time and I decide that's the one. It's a pretty floor-length gown and will look great with my new silver shimmery shoes.

I head into the bathroom that is now fully stocked with my personal items. I have agreed to move in with Logan since Sadie has moved out and I'm not comfortable living alone. Logan emailed my landlord and told her to bill him for the thirty day notice and he would take care of it. Now we have to figure out what to do with the furniture but all my clothes and stuff are now here.

I turn on the water and jump into the shower, carefully shaving all my bits for a romantic night with Logan. We have packed clothes to change into when we get to his club. I told him if it was busy and he needed me to, I would jump in and help out. Mitch was pissed when I called him and told him I wasn't coming back, but I didn't want to face the bar again, especially since he didn't even ban the loser who attacked me.

I slip on a sexy matching red thong and bra set that Logan had the personal shopper deliver. The funny thing is, he picked all these nice matching sets, but when he rips my thong off it leaves me with only the bra so I'm not sure what the point is. I slip on my robe and head back into the bathroom to do my hair and makeup for tonight. I carefully curl and pin my hair and put on some makeup, giving myself smoky eyes, and red lipstick. I step into my shoes and head downstairs to see if Logan is ready. He was going to shower in the guest bathroom so he wouldn't interrupt me getting ready. When I get to the bottom of the stairs, Logan comes around the corner.

"Sweet Jesus, woman, you look incredible."

I blush and look down at the floor. "You look pretty hot yourself." I grasp the collar of his suit coat and pull him toward me.

He kisses my cheek. "I don't want to mess up your makeup. Let's go. We need to head downstairs before I rip that dress off you and we never make it to the show."

"What is it with you and ripping things?" I ask as we head out the main doors.

"Our ride is here," Logan says, leading me to a sleek black limo parked in front of the building.

I look at him in shock. "You got us a limo? How are we getting home from the club later?"

He smiles at me proudly. "Yes, I got us a limo, and my car has been dropped off at the club. The owner of Thrive and the son of an actress cannot show up at one of the hottest art gallery showings of the season driving a car."

He helps me in and slides in beside me. He opens the bottle of champagne in the back of the limo and pours me a glass, then one for himself. "To Sadie and her showing. Let's hope it's a successful night for her."

We clink glasses and take a sip. I instantly relax a little. We arrive at the gallery a short time later and the driver gets out of the car to open the door. Logan climbs out, then tells him to be back by 9:00 so he can take us to the club. When he helps me out, I step onto a red carpet in front of a ton of photographers snapping pictures.

"Mr. Michaels!" one shouts. "Who's this beautiful lady on your arm?"

Logan looks to me with the proudest smile and says, "Skyler Jones, my girlfriend."

Being the son of an actress, I should have expected that he's probably known to reporters. We hear some more shouting.

"Mr. Michaels! Mr. Michaels!"

"Ladies and gentlemen," Logan says, "tonight is about a dear friend of ours, Sadie Johansen, who happens to be exhibiting in this show. Please excuse us so we can enjoy our night."

We walk into the gallery away from the majority of the reporters. There are more inside, but they're covering the art show and are the only ones allowed in. We're asked to pose for a few more photos and then Sadie and Jonah are at our side. We all hug and shake hands. Sadie is bouncing off the walls with excitement.

"Logan dropped your name as an artist to the reporters outside," I comment. "I thought that was pretty cool." She giggles like a school girl.

"Mr. Michaels, can I get a picture with you and your guests?" a reporter asks.

The four of us get together for a picture, and when we are done Logan informs him that Sadie has artwork in the show, that Jonah is her fiancé, and I'm his girlfriend. The reporter asks Sadie to show him her work and she walks off to do her thing. Logan and I stay behind with Jonah.

"Thanks for dropping Sadie's name, Logan," Jonah says. "She's so excited to be here and it will help her career a lot if she can sell a few pieces tonight."

"No problem, glad to help." Logan turns to me. "Should we look around?"

"Do you guys want me to show you where Sadie's stuff is?" Jonah asks.

Logan puts his hand out. "Lead the way."

We head to the back wall where they have eight different pieces that are displayed.

"She's quite good," I remark.

Logan looks them over and nods. "I agree, I like that one." He points to a picture that is a distant image of the two mountains behind the airport with some palm trees in front of them and the sun rising behind them.

"It's beautiful," I say in agreement.

The curator is walking by, and Logan tells her he wants that one.

"Sure thing, please follow me," the woman says, and he follows her to pay for the painting.

"How are you two doing?" Jonah asks me once Logan is out of earshot.

"We're doing well actually. I'm a little nervous about starting at the club though. We're going to head there tonight from here, and I told him I would jump in and help if he needed it. I'm pretty anxious to prove myself to the staff."

"You'll do fine, and if anyone gives you crap you let either me or Shane know and we'll handle it.

"Listen, Jonah I know you're probably worried about Logan knowing I don't do well in relationships, but I want you to know that we have talked about it quite a bit and I don't plan on screwing this one up. He's good to me and I love him."

"Good, glad to hear it. You deserve a good man, and I hope you two have many years of happiness."

I give him a warm smile. "Thanks."

Logan is back and I can't believe it's already getting close to nine. I barely got to talk to Sadie at all, but I'm happy that the curator has marked *'sold'* on two of Sadie's paintings.

"Did you buy two, I ask Logan?"

He grins. "No, the guy behind me wanted the same one I did. Since I had already bought it, he bought his second favorite before that one disappeared too."

The limo pulls up as we are walking outside, and

the photographers are back at it.

"Mr. Michaels, did your friend sell any of her paintings?"

Logan pulls me to his side and smiles for the camera. "She has already sold two but the night is young. She's quite talented and I'm sure she'll sell the remainder of them."

"Mr. Michaels, are you off to another event tonight?"

"No, I'm off to my new club, Thrive. It's doing well and I want to see that it continues to do so."

The driver opens the door for me and I climb in with Logan right behind me.

***

Logan

"They are savages, all of them," I say once the limo door is closed behind us. "It's the one part of being me I hate. The media always wants to know what I'm doing and it's annoying as hell."

Skyler beams at me proudly. "You handle them well, Logan. I'm impressed."

I lean in to kiss her. "Thank you."

I kiss her softly, but it quickly turns into more as our tongues go to war with each other. My hand is squeezing her breast through her dress. "You look amazing and I've wanted to fuck you since you walked down those stairs."

She's nibbling my neck as I say it and it's driving me wild.

She bites my ear and says, "We will be at the

club any minute."

"Good, because I'm going to do something I've never done before."

"What's that?"

I look her in the eyes. "I'm going to bend you over my desk and bury myself balls deep inside you."

The limo comes to a stop and the driver opens the door. I help her out and get our bags. I head straight to my office, not even bothering to ask if my staff needs anything. I shut and lock the door and as soon as I do I push Skyler against it, kissing her hard. Our teeth crash and our tongues slide against one another's. I pull her away from the door slightly so I can unzip her dress and it falls to the floor in a pool at her feet. As soon as it does, she's standing in front of me wearing these sexy silver heels with a matching red thong and bra set.

"I wanted to rip the dress off you but will settle for the panties." I tear them off her and throw them on my desk. "I'm going to fuck you over my desk wearing those heels. I hope you're ready."

Skyler nods, biting her lip. I drag her to my desk and push her down so her stomach is flat on my desk. I insert two fingers into her to confirm she's ready and by God she's so wet for me.

"Please, Logan, I want you inside me." I reach around her with my other hand and rub her clit as she's riding my fingers. "Oh my God, Logan, please tell me I can cum."

I smile proudly that she asked for permission.

"Give it to me, Skyler," I say, and just like that she comes on my fingers. I love the feeling of her pussy clenching shut tight around me as she comes.

She goes to stand up and I slap her ass. "I'm not done. Are you ready to feel my cock in you?"

"Yes please, Logan, give me more!" I ram into her so hard her body shifts on my desk. I can't control myself. She looks so hot spread out naked on my desk in these heels. I continue to slam into her, fucking her harder than I ever have. She's moaning and whimpering as I work her back up to an orgasm. I reach my hand around to play with her clit so I can get her there faster. I have been semi-hard all night watching her walk around in that dress imagining this moment. I know she's getting close because I can feel her holding on for me. She's waiting for me to give her permission. She's tightening her muscles around my cock and I have to give her the okay because if not I'm going to explode before her.

"Come with me," I grunt, and she lets it go, milking me and screaming my name. "That was incredible," I tell her as I lay over her for a moment to catch my breath.

We both quickly clean up and get dressed so I can see what's going on out in the club. Jonah is off tonight so I want to be sure there are no issues with either the bartenders or the bouncers. As soon as we're on the floor, I see Troy walking through the club.

"What are you doing back in my club and how did you get in?"

"I'm here for my last paycheck and to ask you to drop the charges so I'll be able to find another job."

"How did you get in?"

"I told the rookie bouncer at the door I was here to see you about my last paycheck and that he had to let me in. I told him I'd call the police."

"Get out! I owe you nothing for your final paycheck. You drank it all in the liquor you stole. And if you come here again I'll have you arrested for trespassing. You've been blacklisted from most of the local clubs. Not being able to get a job has nothing to do with your charges. You'll never work in a club again."

"You can't fucking do that!"

"I can and I already did. Now you have thirty seconds to leave before I call the police and you spend another weekend in jail."

"You'll be hearing from my fucking lawyer."

I look him dead in the eye. "I look forward to it."

Kelly comes over just then. "Hey, Skyler. I know you aren't scheduled tonight, but Shawna is out back puking her brains out. Can you jump in?"

"Sure." Skyler follows Kelly behind the bar, where Kelly quickly shows her the register and how to set up a tab.

In minutes Skyler is going to town making drinks and running the bar with Kelly. I'm so proud of her. I walk over to bar two and ask if they need any help. The bartender informs me they are low on Sam Adams bottles. I run to the back, sign out a case and then head to the main bar to see what they need. I don't know why but this place is jamming tonight and I don't mind helping out one bit.

"Do you ladies need anything?" I ask.

"I need a bottle of Malibu and a bottle of Absolut!" Skyler yells and then Kelly says, "I need more Bud."

I head to the back again to get what they need and take it back to the main bar. Skyler is wiping down the bar while Kelly runs glasses through the washer. I make a mental note that they're a good team. I'll have to pair them up more. I walk to the entrance and see there's a line down the street to get into the club and I'm thrilled. It's only 11:00 and the club is packed with many others clamoring to get in.

"Hey, Nick," I ask, "did you let Troy into the club?"

"Yeah, sorry. I didn't know what to do. I knew you weren't on a walkie yet because your limo only pulled up about fifteen minutes before he got here and I hadn't heard you check in. I didn't know what to do. He was threatening to call the cops and I didn't want trouble at the club."

"It's fine, but listen; next time he shows up here, you tell him to call the cops and then you call either me, Shane, or Jonah. Do not let him in the club."

"Got it. Sorry, Logan, it won't happen again."

I find Shane behind the main bar helping Kelly and Skyler. I head to the back to get Sky an ear wig since she's on the clock.

***

The night has finally come to an end and the bar is empty. Skyler and Kelly make everyone their one drink on me so they can unwind after a busy night. Pretty much everyone has stuck around. They're all laughing and having a good time.

133

"Yo!" Kelly shouts out. "If you were worried about this chick holding her own, you can stop. She kicked ass tonight." She gives Skyler a high five and hugs her. "She wasn't even scheduled to work, but we were hurting and she jumped in and owned it. Thanks for covering, girl!"

Skyler blushes slightly as she smiles at her new friend. "Any time. Glad I was here to help."

Shane tells Skyler, "Nice job tonight. I jumped behind the bar to make sure you weren't screwing up or getting behind and you did great!"

From the smile on her face, I bet her confidence increased tenfold.

Chapter 10

Logan

Tonight is opening night for the singles event. Skyler is in my office changing into her dress for the night and she's a nervous wreck. I keep trying to tell her she'll be fine but it's hard to sing in front of people you know hoping they are going to like you. At this point I'm glad I didn't tell her that my friend Mikey will be here to watch her for a possible gig in between singing at Thrive. Although she said she had fun behind the bar the other night, I think she could care less at this point.

I knock on the door because I want her to do a mic check before we open the club. She opens the door.

"Sweetie, you look amazing."

"Thanks!"

"Are you ready to do a sound check?" I ask, and she follows me out to the floor.

Shane sees her first. "Looking good, Sky. You're going to kill it tonight."

She smiles shyly at him and gives a quick thanks as she continues toward the stage. She walks up, clips her ear bud into her ear, and takes the mic. After speaking into it, she asks me to turn it down a few notches. I do and she tries again. She sings into the mic and I swear everyone in the club stops to listen to her because she's that good.

"Logan, I think it's still a bit loud for the crowd you're going to have. What do you think?"

I turn down the speakers a bit more. She sings a few notes and stops. "That's better, no?" she asks, and I give her thumbs up.

She walks over the bar. "Kelly, can I have two waters with lemon, one for now and one for the stage?"

"You got it." Kelly hands her the two glasses.

Jonah takes the glass for the stage from the bar and puts it up on the stool we have set up for her.

"Okay everyone, listen up. This is our first ever singles night. We have no idea how this is going to go, but there is a line out the door and the VIP sections are all booked so it seems like it's going to go pretty well so far. The food is out, Skyler is ready to go. Bouncers, you know your positions right?" They all nod. "Good. Make sure you keep an eye out. No one gets on the stage and make sure that tip vase doesn't disappear. Now let's get this place opened!"

Nick heads to the door with a few other team members to open the club doors. People start flowing in and Skyler is up on stage singing away. There are menus on all the tables offering wine with their prices. Kelly is walking around with a small bar tray and a pad to write down what people would like to order. I've informed the bouncers I want all VIPs escorted to their tables and to call me when one arrives.

I'm in a daze watching Skyler sing when I hear in my ear, "Logan, you there?"

I press my button to respond. "Yeah. What's up?"

"There is a guy named Mikey here to see you. He says he has a VIP section reserved."

I smile. It's time for my girl to shine. "I'll be right there."

When I reach the front door, I see my friend. "Mikey, my man. How's it going?" We man hug and I welcome him into my club. "Come on, I'll show you to your table and your drinks are on me tonight."

He pats my back. "This club looks awesome, Logan. You did a great job, and I love the idea of this singles night."

I'm showing him to his seat, and halfway there I hear in my ear that there is another VIP at the door. I notice Mikey is looking up at the stage. "Excuse me one minute." I hit the button on my ear bud. "Shane, there is a VIP at the door. Can you escort them in?"

"You got it. On my way."

"Is that her?" Mikey asks with a huge smile on his face.

"That's her," I respond, looking so proud. My girl looks beautiful and sounds fantastic.

Mikey looks at me, back at her, then back to me. "Damn, bro, she's hot! How the hell did you find her?"

"She came walking into my club with a friend of hers one night. Remember, you can have her to sing in your club but that is it. She's mine, so hands off."

He laughs. "She's good. I'd love to put her into rotation at my club."

"You've hardly heard her sing."

"I've been in the music business long enough to know talent when I see it. She's in." We shake hands and walk the rest of the way to his VIP section, where he takes a seat and orders a drink. I had each VIP section set up with their own cheese and cracker station so they don't have to get up and fight with the rest of the club, and I informed Kelly that he's a special guest and to give me the bill for his drinks for the night.

***

Skyler

It's finally time for me to take a break. I have been singing on stage for almost two hours, and I need to drink some water and give my voice a rest.

"Thank you, ladies and gentlemen. I'll be back with more shortly." I walk off the stage and Logan is there to meet me. He gives me a kiss and tells me I'm doing an amazing job. The vase he left is filling up with tips and people look like they are having a great time.

"Come with me. I have someone I want you to meet." He takes my hand and leads me to the VIP section. Kelly is there serving them their drinks and

I ask her for a tall glass of water with lemon as we cross paths. She nods on her way out the room and heads straight to the bar.

"Mikey, this is my girlfriend Skyler. Skyler, my friend Mikey. Honey, this is the club owner I was telling you about and he would like to add you to the live entertainment rotation at his club."

I have a huge smile on my face. "Are you serious?"

He shakes her hand and says, "Very serious. I can't believe someone hasn't scooped you up for a better deal. You have a fantastic voice." Kelly returns with my water, and we relax and talk about music and my background, which to be honest isn't much other than I enjoy singing and have done it all my life.

"I would like to bring you into my club right away. What is your schedule like?"

"The other gig I work is a crappy one that I'll give up in a heartbeat to work for you. The only night I'm not free is every other Wednesday because I'll be singing here."

"Good," Mikey says enthusiastically, "because I want you on Thursday nights starting a week from tomorrow."

I'm beaming at this point. "That sounds good to me. I'll add it to my calendar as soon as I'm done working. What time do you need me at the club?"

"Eight-thirty will be fine. We have pretty much the same equipment as here so I'll need you to do a quick sound check and then start singing when we open."

"Great! Well, it was nice meeting you, but I need

to get back on stage." I stand and shake his hand. Logan takes my hand and walks me back to the stage.

He has a huge smile on his face when he says, "Told you he would love you."

"I'm so excited. Thank you so much for everything you have done for me." I start to head back on stage and I stop short when I see who is in the crowd. It's Billy from the bar and I don't know what to do. I don't have an ear wig to quietly report him to Logan and the rest of the team, and clearly they do not recognize him because they haven't moved in to remove him. I sing my first song, keeping an eye on him without making eye contact with him because I do not want him to know that I know he's there.

I start singing the next song, and while I do I'm trying to remain calm but think of how I can warn Logan that he's here. He hasn't left his spot. He's standing there drooling, staring at me like I'm a piece of meat. I'm doing my best to continue singing without giving it away that I'm scared, but the way he's standing there staring at me is giving me the creeps.

I need to take a break after the next song, because if I don't I'm going to blow my career right here and now. I refuse to do that. Looking around, I don't see Logan anywhere. I wish I could make eye contact with him so I could try to signal him but I can't, and Jonah's back is to me so he won't see me. I don't want patrons to panic when I don't know what Billy's intentions are. After I finish the song I'm singing, there is a round of applause and I again thank everyone.

"Thank you very much. I apologize, but I need to take one more quick break and I'll be back with you to finish the night off. I hope you're all enjoying yourselves." I walk down the few stairs of the stage and Jonah is by my side, then Logan is running toward me.

"What's wrong, Skyler?" Jonah asks.

"He was here."

"Who was here?" Logan asks with concern.

"Billy. The guy who attacked me. I saw him in the crowd and I couldn't get anyone's attention. He was just standing there staring at me. It was freaking me out."

"Let's take a break out back for a second and I'll scan the tapes to see if we can spot him." We head to Logan's office and I show him who Billy is, but he's no longer standing there. Logan quickly texts each of the bouncers his picture and says be on the lookout for him, that if he's spotted to call Logan immediately. He gets thumbs up emojis from each bouncer and we head back out to the stage.

I'm finally singing the last song of the night, and I give the crowd a big smile and thank them all for coming. I receive a huge round of applause and it feels great.

"Thank you, everyone! Have a great night and drive safely!" I head off stage and Logan is there again to meet me.

"He isn't here, sweetie. We scoured the club. He must have left when he saw you come off stage for the second time."

"Thank you for looking out for me." I'm

141

freaking out inside, but I don't want to tell Logan that because he won't want me to sing at Mikey's club. He walks me back to his office so I can change into my more comfortable clothes, and when we get back out front the cleanup has begun.

Both Logan and I chip in getting things squared away so the staff can have their drink and we can head home. It has been a long, busy night and we are all pretty tired. After we get things ready for tomorrow, Logan calls everyone around the bar. He and I make everyone's drinks and hand them out.

"You guys did a kick ass job tonight," Logan says. "We were slammed and I'm glad I went on the heavier side with staff because we could have been screwed. That said, we will not be going lighter on staff next week, so I'll see you all back here. Our entertainment will be different, but Skyler will be here with me so if you need back up you'll have it. The crowd clearly loved her so we'll have her back the following week to sing again and I'll have a different backup plan if need be."

Everyone is hooting and hollering for me, and I start to blush as usual. "Thanks, guys." I try to sound as confident as possible, though I'm not sure I succeed.

"Alright, everyone, let's finish up so we can all get out of here. Tomorrow night is Thirsty Thursday and another busy night for us."

"It was pumping in here tonight, huh?" I ask Logan.

"We were busier tonight than we have been on 18+ night in a long time. Now we have to see if it stays that way."

"I'm proud of you. You did an amazing job at planning and promoting this event. It's a success because of your hard work."

"Thanks, sweetie. Now let's kick all the staff out so we can get home."

I laugh. "Okay."

"Everyone, it's time to get out of here!" he shouts to his crew. They all hand their glasses to Kelly or toss the bottles in the trash. Everyone heads out, and Logan and I grab the last trash bag and head out the door. After locking up, we walk to his car, and the sight we find isn't what we expect.

His car has been trashed, and I mean totally smashed up. Windows are broken, headlights shattered, taillights broken, dents everywhere, like someone took a bat to his car. He calls the police from his cell phone. While we wait he calls his limo driver to come back to the club to pick us up.

We head back into the club to wait for the police, heading straight to Logan's office to check out the security footage. He finds the camera covering his car and he can see the figure walking around it. He's definitely carrying some sort of metal object, probably a bat. He's bashing the shit out of the car, but because it's dark and he's wearing a hoodie, you can't make out who it is.

I feel bad, like this is my fault. "I'm sorry, Logan. I hope this wasn't that ass from the bar."

Logan shakes his head. "He wouldn't know my car unless he has been watching us. I think it was Troy. He wanted me to drop the charges against him so he could get another job and I threw him out."

I start pacing because my gut somehow says this

was Billy.

"Troy wasn't wearing a hoodie when he came in; was Billy?"

Skyler shrugs. "No."

"That doesn't mean he didn't ditch it before he came in." Logan makes a copy of the tape to hand over to the police, and when we walk outside with it they're arriving, as is our limo. I head to the car to wait while he deals with the police. It only takes him about five minutes before he joins me and we're on our way home.

Chapter 11

Skyler

I'm meeting up for lunch with Sadie today, and I'm so excited. I haven't seen her much since the art show and while I was there I didn't even get to talk to her. It feels like forever since I have seen her. So much has happened since then. I can't wait to catch up and I miss my friend. I'm sitting in our favorite diner waiting for her, and she's running late. I sip my diet soda and watch out the window for her when I see her finally pull in and hustle into the diner.

"I'm so sorry I'm late. There's a major accident and it has everything backed up for miles."

I stand to hug her. "No worries. I was sipping some soda waiting for you. I miss you so much, Sadie. I don't get to see you now that you moved in with Jonah."

"I know. Things with Jonah and me are great, but now that we're planning the wedding it's even crazier." She rolls her eyes as she shows me the binder of wedding stuff she wants to talk about later. "How are things with Logan going?"

"Great. But first I want to know all about the art show."

She glows as she tells me how wonderful it was. "We had the best night. All of my paintings have sold and I've had people contact me to find out when I'll have more up at the gallery."

"That is so awesome! I'm so happy for you!"

"Did you know Logan bought one of my paintings?"

"I did. We were looking at them together and talking about them and he really liked the one he picked. As a matter of fact, the guy behind him in line wanted it too, but Logan beat him to it so the other guy bought his second favorite of your paintings."

"How cool is that!" she squeals.

The waitress comes over to take her drink order and hands Sadie a menu. I already know what I want, and if I know Sadie she'll be getting a bacon cheeseburger and fries.

"I'm so happy for you, Sadie. Have you been busy painting?"

"Yeah, but I also pulled some of my art from the smaller galleries and put them in the bigger one until I can get some more work done. There'll be another show in two months and they want me to have more pieces ready so I have to stay focused. So what's going on with you and Logan?"

"Well, we've pretty much been living together since the attack, even though I didn't give up the apartment right away. Things are going well. He gets me, and it's like he can read me. He knows if something is bothering me and he's good about getting me to open up."

"That's awesome. I'm so glad I dragged you out with me that night."

"Me too, because I have seriously fallen in love with him. I haven't told him yet but I totally will."

"What do you mean you haven't told him?"

"We were having this conversation at the house and he told me he loved me, but I didn't say it back. Then later that day I explained to him that I didn't say it because I wanted him to know I was saying it because I meant it not because he said it. He seemed quite happy with that and we dropped it." The waitress returns with Sadie's soda and we place our orders. I ordered a Rueben and she ordered a bacon cheese burger like I thought she would.

"What kind of wedding info have you started collecting?" I'm secretly hoping she isn't going to turn into bridezilla or make us wear ugly dresses.

"I have collected pictures of dresses I like, hall decor, DJ names, florists, and stuff like that. Jonah swears he can get the DJ from the club, but I don't know how he'll do that when he's at the club on Saturday nights." She makes a disgusted face. "Oh yeah, Jonah told me that the creep who attacked you showed up at the club the other night."

"Yeah. What Jonah doesn't know is that someone bashed in Logan's car that same night and we don't know if it was Billy, since we saw him at the club, or Troy, since he's pissed at Logan for not dropping the charges. Not knowing which one it was is killing me."

"Oh my god, no way! That would totally freak me out! Was Logan pissed about his car?"

The waitress returns with our food and tells us she'll be back to check on us shortly. I continue with my story while we eat.

"Nah, he has insurance and it isn't like he can't afford another one. The thing was destroyed, headlights, windows, taillights, everything. Someone pretty much took a metal bat to it and beat every inch of his car. He called the police and arranged for his limo driver to come back for us and take us home from the club."

I start blushing thinking about the amazing sex we had in the limo on the way home.

"What are you thinking about?" Sadie asks, shoving her burger in her mouth.

"What? Nothing." I shove a french fry in my mouth so I can think of something to change the subject.

"Bullshit. You were biting your lip, and red is creeping up your neck."

I give her a sideways grin and drop my voice so no one will hear. "We had the most explosive sex in the back of his limo on the way home."

She laughs at me. "I would never say this in front of Jonah but Logan looks like he's pretty killer in the sheets."

"In the sheets, on the couch, in the office, in a limo, it doesn't matter where it is, he's incredible." I smile and add, "He always takes care of me first, and that's something I have never had before."

"That *is* awesome!" Sadie smiles back at me, and I can tell she's genuinely excited for me. "I'm glad that Jonah and I still have good sex, because I don't know what I would do if it faded."

"I can't see anything changing with Logan and me either, and our schedules are so great, especially now that I work at the club with him. We get our time apart when I'm off, but when I'm working I still get to see him and I have him take me home after work so I'll never be alone. I can't believe we've been seeing each other for a few months already. Time is moving quickly, especially now that we have set a routine."

The waitress comes to remove our plates and asks if we want another round of drinks. We both say, "Yes please," and Sadie flips the binder open. The first thing she has in the binder is the different locations that she would like to get married and different color options she would like.

"I'm thinking about a spring wedding, and if I can line up a place I'll do it this coming spring because Jonah and I want to be married sooner rather than later. Jonah is asking Logan to be his best man today." She shows me the coral color dresses she's thinking she'll probably go with.

As we're talking, I have a strange feeling, like someone is watching us. I look up around the diner and see nothing until movement outside catches my eye.

"Oh my god, he's here." I grab my phone.

Sadie says, "Who?"

I casually nod toward the window. "Look at my car." Logan's phone rings; he answers right away. "Hey, sweetie, what's up?"

"Logan, he's here leaning on my car. He knows

my car."

"Shit! You're at Trisha's right?" He's trying to sound calm, but there is panic in his voice because we're basically sitting ducks.

"Yeah, Sadie and I are inside."

"Don't leave the diner. And call the cops. We're on our way."

"Okay, we'll wait for you to get here."

I hang up and call John, the police officer that came the night Billy attacked me, since he gave me his card. I inform him that Billy is leaning against my car and has been stalking me. I tell him about how I saw him in the club while I was onstage but didn't report it because, despite being on camera, he got away. He tells me to hold on for a second while he calls for backup and to keep an eye out in case he leaves. They need to know what he's driving.

"Sadie, Jonah and Logan are on their way. They want us to stay in here. We're all going to go to Logan's and hang there where they can keep us safe."

"I have a good mind to go out there and kick this guy's ass."

"You tell her to stay put and do not go anywhere near him!" John yells into the phone, apparently hearing Sadie's comment. "What if he's armed?"

"John heard you and is yelling for you to stay in the diner, so stop," I say to Sadie, then address John. "He's getting in a beat up pick-up truck. It looks like a Ford, two doors, and it's a dull black. It looks pretty old, but I have no idea what year it is. He's driving toward the building with no front plate so I have no idea what else to give you. He drove around the back of the diner to leave. He must have seen me on the phone."

"I'm almost at the diner now. Stay put until Logan gets there, and I'll try to catch up with him. I'll call you guys a little later to update you."

"Thank you, John." I end the call. "He said he's almost here and he's going to go after him. wants us to stay put until Logan and Jonah get here."

"We might as well look at the binder some more and talk about ideas." She flips the page.

"Have you called any of these locations to see if they are available and get pricing?"

Sadie shakes her head. "I was hoping maybe you would help me with that."

"Sure. We can call as soon as we get to my place. That way you can print them out and see what's in your budget and what isn't."

"My parents said they would give us money toward the wedding though they can't afford to pay for it all, so we have to make sure the place isn't crazy. We aren't having a huge wedding since neither of our families is big, but still this is LA. Everything is expensive. Unless you're rich and famous, then they give it away, which never made sense to me, by the way. You're rich so you can afford anything, but because they want you at their location they'll give it to you for free just to say you got married there."

I roll my eyes at her. "They should charge them so they can afford to give better rates to us poor people."

Sadie bursts out laughing. "If only!"

A moment later Logan and Jonah come running

through the door like we were under attack and they had to protect us. "Where is he?" he asks, panting like they ran a marathon.

"He left in a black pick-up truck while I was on the phone with John. He went to follow him and asked us to stay here until you guys got here. He said he would call us later with an update."

"Okay ladies, let's get out of here so we can get home and you two can continue planning Jonah's funeral."

"Screw you, man," Jonah says, nudging his arm angrily.

"Wait, Logan, I haven't paid the bill." I nod over to my waitress, who brings the bill over.

Logan hands her a fifty, telling her to keep the change. We head out to my car and find my tires are slashed. Logan makes a call to have my car towed and my tires replaced before we head back to his house.

"We're going to drop Sadie's car off at our place and then we will head to yours," Jonah tells us.

"Cool. We'll get some takeout for dinner later," Logan calls to him as I get in his car.

"I'm glad you called me as soon as you spotted him," he says when he gets in.

"It was weird, Logan. I had this feeling of being watched, and when I looked outside there he was, leaning against my car. I hadn't even noticed he slashed my tires."

He glances at me quickly. "Don't worry about the tires. They'll be replaced and your car will be back at the house tomorrow."

"Thanks, Logan."

He gives me a sideways grin. "It's no problem, love."

I can't help but grin. That is the first time he has called me that.

"I have to admit this guy is starting to creep me out a bit, and now that he knows my car I can't help but wonder if he bashed your car too." I shake my head. "I hate we don't know if it was him or Troy."

"I know, and I promise I'm doing what I can to figure that out."

I look out the window, trying to think about why he would be doing this. I mean seriously, telling a guy to keep his hands to himself is hardly a big deal to be carrying on this way. There has to be more to it. I try to think about how long this guy was hanging in the bar and if I could have done something more to piss him off, but I'm not sure. I know he'd been hanging around with his friends for a while and they get pretty drunk on sports nights. As a matter of fact, I cut off one of his friends one night because he was drunk and being obnoxious, but I don't think I'd ever cut him off other than the night he attacked me.

"What are you thinking?" Logan asks, drawing my attention back to him.

"I'm trying to figure out why this guy is doing this. Clearly there has to be more to it than I shut him off and told him to keep his hands to himself. It wouldn't make sense for him to continue carrying on like this over something simple like that. I also don't believe he doesn't remember anything from the night before. I think that's a crock of shit and he just said that to make it look like a drunken accident."

"You're right, but unfortunately until the cops do their digging, we have no idea why he's doing this. Have you ever noticed him at any of the clubs you sing at?"

I stop to think for a moment. "No, but with the lighting it isn't always easy to clearly see faces. He could hide out in a corner of the room and I would never see him. I can't help but think there's more to this, and I wish I knew what it was."

We pull up to the building and get out of the car. As we approach Greg, Logan lets him know we have guests coming and they'll be arriving shortly. He tells us to have a nice evening as we head toward the elevators.

Once we are inside I head straight for the fridge and pour myself a glass of Moscato. I don't usually drink this early in the day, but my nerves are on edge and I need to relax. I'm finally going to have a night with our friends relaxing in our home, and I want to be able to enjoy myself.

Logan walks up to me, taking my glass and placing it on the counter. "You know I'll keep you safe right?" I look to the floor for a moment. "Skyler, look at me."

He raises my chin so I'm forced to look at him and he kisses me gently, never taking his eyes off mine. "I love you and I'm not going to let anything happen to you. If I have to hire security for when I'm not around I will, but we're almost always together so don't stress it, okay?"

"And who is going to protect you? What if he comes after you, Logan? I can't stand the thought."

"Listen to me, love. If things start to get out of control, I'll get security for both of us. If that's what it takes to make you feel safe and you'll be happy then that's what I'll do. For now let's wait to see what John says when he calls a bit later."

He kisses me a bit more passionately this time and then gives me the big hug I need. The phone rings and it's Greg letting us know our guests have arrived and are on their way up. Sadie and I hug and Jonah and Logan shake hands. I offer Sadie some wine since I'm drinking already and I offer Jonah a beer. They both accept and I hand them their drinks. Sadie and I take our drinks and head to the balcony to look over the rest of the binder. She picks up where she left off with flowers and dress ideas and so on. We make a few phone calls to see who has availability for the spring and get some prices.

As we are calling around, we find a few places do have a weekend or two open for the spring and can squeeze in her small wedding though she'll need to make a decision quickly. One of the locations is way out of her budget so she rips it from her binder and crumples it up. Two are perfect for her budget and she made an appointment to go see them this week. The last one was slightly out of her budget but she figures if these two suck she can probably make it work.

"I may have to beg Daddy for a little more money." She winks at me and giggles.

"You know your parents will give it to you. We have made good progress. Let's take a break and get some more wine. Then we can see what the guys are up to."

***

Logan

"Fuck me," I mumble to John when Skyler and Sadie come walking back in. They have the worst timing, because I didn't want Sky hearing this conversation.

"Um, that's my job," she says jokingly.

Jonah turns around and mouths to her, "It's John."

Her eyes grow wide because she knows I'm talking about her stalker, and I'm sure she can tell I'm ready to explode. She walks to the kitchen to pour herself and Sadie some more wine as I hang up the phone.

"You do not leave this house alone, am I clear?"

She nods. "What is going on?"

"The police lost him earlier but got a warrant for his arrest. They went to his house and found a Skyler shrine in his apartment. He has pictures of you singing in clubs, working behind the bar, going in and out of my place. Apparently he's an alcoholic who has been sentenced to rehab twice now. One of the times he was in rehab Troy was with him, so now we don't know who bashed my car or if they are in this together."

I can see she's visibly shaken. She downs her wine.

"How long has this guy been following me?"

"It doesn't matter. When the police catch him he'll be going to jail for a long time. This isn't something we need to think about right now. We have friends here and we need to decide on some dinner so we can relax a bit, okay?"

Sadie takes her hand and pulls her to the couch to try and get her mind off things, and I'm glad because I need to talk to Jonah.

"You need to know he had pictures of you too. They were more recent. I'm assuming he knows it's you that kicked his ass outside the bar that night, so watch your back because he may be gunning for you."

"Thanks for the heads up, but I'll be fine. I have a license to carry. I'll start using it."

"I'm setting up security for Sky. Do you want me to set it up for you guys too?"

"Was Sadie in any of the pics?"

I shake my head. "No, it was you, me, and a shit ton of Skyler. This guy is obsessed with her."

I hate that Skyler is living in fear over what will happen next in her life and I need to do everything I can to protect her. That means making some calls first thing in the morning to find a good security detail for her.

"Let's go figure out what the girls feel like ordering for dinner."

We walk over to the couch with beers in hand.

"Ladies, what would you like for dinner? I have a ton of takeout menus in the kitchen."

They both reply at the same time, "Chinese food," and Jonah and I crack up laughing.

"Yeah, they're not best friends, are they?"

"Hey, welcome to my world, Logan." I walk into the kitchen to get the menu for my favorite Chinese take-out and hand it over so they can decide what they want to eat.

***

It's pretty late, and Jonah and Sadie are heading out, which is perfectly fine with me. I want to take my girl upstairs and make sweet love to her. I'm hoping she'll fall asleep and dream of me after and not the psycho following her. The girls say their goodbyes and we make a promise to get together like this weekly to hang out outside of work. Once they're out the door and I lock up, I walk toward Skyler, who has headed into the kitchen to put her glass in the sink.

"You ready for bed?" I ask, gliding my hand across her cheek and tucking a strand of her beautiful light brown hair behind her ear.

"Absolutely."

From her smile I know we're on the same page. I take her hand and pull her toward the stairs. She runs up them to our room and I follow behind her, checking out her ass. She has the most gorgeous ass.

When I get to the top of the stairs she's standing against the pole of my bed in nothing but her thong and her bra. I lean against the door frame. "You should have removed the thong too," I say with a laugh. "You know I'm only going to rip it off."

She chuckles and tries to remove them.

"It's too late." I walk toward her slowly like she's my prey. I kiss her hard, seeing her standing here wanting me has me hard as a rock.

I skim my fingers across the waistband of her

158

thong and she braces herself for the rip, which never comes. I lean into her neck and take in her scent, licking her from her collarbone to her ear. My hand is sliding up her stomach to her breast. I pull it out so it's pushed up over the top of her bra and pinch her nipple hard. She moans as I nibble on her ear. I kiss my way to the other side of her neck so I can free her other breast. I pinch her nipple and she winces, her nipple pebbling under my assault. Her head goes back and her eyes close as she takes in the sensation of my hands on her body. I lean down to take her nipple in my mouth, sucking on it hard while I grab her ass and press her into my erection.

I know she's wet for me and I need to taste her. I walk her to the side of the bed and push her down, grabbing the strap of her panties so they shred as she falls. She laughs and I toss them aside.

Once she straightens herself out on the bed, I climb between her legs and start lapping up her juices. I could drink her for days. She's moaning and grinding her hips.

"Skyler, lie still. This is your only warning. I'll tie you down if I need to."

She freezes in place, remembering who is in charge in the bedroom. I kiss the inside of each of her legs before I make my way back to her hardened nub. I start licking it slowly, savoring her taste. I know it's killing her to lay still. I can feel her fighting it and it makes me laugh. I start licking her harder and insert two fingers deep inside of her. I want to see how good she can do at not coming until I tell her to. I work her hard and fast.

"Logan, please, can I come?"

I pull my lips from her clit. "No. Don't you dare come yet. I'm not done tasting you." I stop my fingers while I speak to give her a minute to calm back down, then work at her hard and fast again. My fingers are fucking her deep and my tongue is all over her. I take her nub in my mouth and suck on it hard, rubbing my tongue over the tip of it.

"Logan, please! I can't hold on much longer."

I stop again, though this time my fingers are still buried deep inside her, fingering her.

"You'll wait until I tell you to come or you'll be punished." I can feel her muscles tightening as she's fighting the urge and I have to admit I'm pretty impressed. I lower my face to her one more time, removing my fingers so I can rub her clit with my thumb. My tongue is buried deep in her as I lick her insides. I know she's about to lose it, so I pull my tongue out. "Go." As soon as my tongue lands on her pussy, she's exploding all over my face and I love it.

I start to kiss my way to her ticklish hips. I love when I nibble her hips. It causes her to giggle; it is the sweetest sound, and it always makes me smile. I stick my tongue out to kiss and lick my way up her stomach to her breasts. I massage one with my hand while I suck on the other. I know she wants to grind her hips against my erection because I can feel her flinch and then fight the urge.

"You make me so proud."

She smiles and blushes.

I climb off her to remove my clothes and while I am I can see her legs sliding around on the bed. I must be getting soft because normally I would tell her she was moving again and I would get something to tie her down, but I want to feel her, and now, so there is no time for that.

I climb back on top of her, look her dead in the eyes, and tell her I love her, then kiss her before she can respond. I don't need her to say it, because I know how she feels about me and me about her.

My kiss is passionate and one full of want and desire. I can't hold out any longer so I slam my rock hard cock deep inside her and hold still for a moment. She moans and whimpers into my mouth. I'm not going to stop kissing her because I love how she tastes and she loves tasting herself on my tongue. I start to move, giving her what she wants. Her hips start meeting my thrusts. I finally pull away from the kiss so I can pull her legs up onto my shoulders and lean forward so I can get even deeper.

"Oh my god, Logan!"

I smile as I pound into her. She can no longer move because I have her pinned down just the way I like it. Her legs are in the air by my ears as I slide my cock in and out of her. She's moaning and screaming my name. I know she wants to come, I can feel her muscles tighten around my cock trying to fight it, and I love how it feels. I pound her a few more times, before I tell her, "Come for me, love."

She lets it go and milks me for every drop I've got. I drop her legs and fall forward, still pumping the last of my seed deep inside of her. I'm panting and exhausted from the stressful few days, but we really needed that. Her eyes are closed and I know she's tired.

"Come on, love. Let's get cleaned up and

161

changed and then I'll hold you while you sleep." She nods, never moving a muscle. I pull her close instead, and we both doze off.

Chapter 12

Logan

"Hey, princess. It's time to wake up," I whisper, rubbing my nose against Skyler's. She grumbles and rolls over. "Oh no you don't." I tickle her and she bursts into a fit of laughter.

"Logan, stop! I hate being tickled!" I keep going until she screams, "Okay! I'm getting up! You need to get off me because I have to pee, and if you keep tickling me you're going to have a wet bed."

I laugh and climb off of her, admiring the view as she goes running off to the bathroom completely naked.

When she walks back into the room and realizes I'm already dressed, she pouts.

"How come you're dressed already? Did I sleep that late?"

"I let you sleep as long as I could, love, but the new security team will be here in about an hour and a half. Then I want to go car shopping."

"You're going to replace your car today?"

163

"And yours. I want you driving something a bit safer. Now please go shower. It's distracting with you standing there in front of me all naked like that. I brought you some coffee," I say, pointing to the cup on the nightstand.

She leans down onto the bed and gives me a kiss. "You're so sweet. Thank you."

"You're welcome!" I call out as she shuts the bathroom door.

I head back downstairs to make her some breakfast. Since I couldn't sleep this morning, I already ate. I was up early after a fucked-up nightmare I had about Sky. I got up and went to work on hiring security and making sure they would be here today. I also sent Jonah a text message this morning to call me when he could. I want to hire two new bouncers to have added security on the weekend and when Skyler is singing. He's probably just waking up, but hopefully he can place the ad today and get on it in the next few days. For now Sky's security guard will have to hang at the club when she's there.

I have my laptop on the counter, confirming our entertainment for tomorrow and telling the caterer to be prepared for a larger crowd this week. I also email an extra bartender to come in and help Kelly manage the VIP sections because they are booked solid again for tomorrow night.

I hear footsteps and I look up from my computer to see sexy legs walking down the stairs. Sky's wearing these short shorts that my personal shopper bought for her and she looks unbelievable; however, I'll need to talk to the shopper about covering her up a bit more. I mean Christ, the woman has a stalker and seeing those legs I can understand why.

"What's wrong, sweetie?" she asks, setting her coffee cup down on the counter.

"Those shorts don't leave much to the imagination."

"Your shopper brought them for me and it's going to be hot today."

She's wearing a tank top and a tight fitted V-neck shirt over it with her hair tied back. Looking at her has given me an instant hard on.

"Love, I think you're trying to kill me. How am I supposed to function with you looking like that?"

She laughs. "Death by hard on," she says.

I swat her ass and tell her it's not funny. We'll see how funny she thinks it is later when I shred those shorts and fuck her over the back of my couch. Better yet, I may fuck her over the back of the couch as soon as security leaves before we go car shopping.

I shake off my thoughts and close my laptop, then get up to toast the bagel I pulled out for her while she makes herself another cup of coffee. She plops down on the barstool and I head to the fridge to pull out some cream cheese, placing it on the counter with a butter knife and her toasted bagel.

My phone rings; it's Jonah.

"I have to take this, love."

I sit on the stool beside her with my coffee. "Jonah, thanks for giving me a call. Listen, I was thinking about it, and I would like for you to hire two new bouncers. Going forward, I want two of you at the door and Skyler's security will be standing by the stage with you during her performances to help keep her safe."

"No problem. I'll run an ad today and get working on it. If it's alright with you I'd like to talk to one of my boys. He just retired from the military and is home for good. He may be looking for a job."

"That sounds good to me."

The house phone rings and Skyler gets up to answer it. I hear her say "Okay, Greg, send him up."

"Jonah, I've got to run. Security is here, but keep me posted."

"Will do. Later, man."

"Later." I cut the call as there's a knock on the door and two guys come walking in. They are both a little bigger than me and both carrying sidearms. One sticks out his hand and says, "Tony." The other does the same. "Jake."

"Thanks for coming on short notice. This is Skyler, my girlfriend and the person you're protecting. I'm Logan, as I'm sure you know."

They both nod at Skyler. "Ma'am."

She takes a deep breath. "Guys, this is only going to work if you call me Sky. I'm way too young to be a ma'am, and if we can't get past that there'll be issues."

I laugh because there are times when my sweet girl is so shy and other times when she's feisty as hell and wants what she wants.

"Please call her Sky. She has enough stress and I don't want her all pissed off because I'm demanding this detail and you guys are constantly calling her ma'am."

They both nod.

"Okay, Sky," Tony says, "tell us about your routine."

"I'm off most Sundays and every Monday and Tuesday. Wednesday through Saturday I'm either singing or bartending at Thrive. I picked up another singing gig that I start this Thursday night at Club Temptation. I sleep most of the morning because I'm up so late. My daytime routine varies, but usually Logan and I are together so he can tell you what your responsibilities will be."

"I'd like one of you nearby at all times so if we want to go out we have a tail keeping an eye on us," I say. "You'll need to be discreet, especially when we're out in public. I'm somewhat known because of my mother, but also as the owner of Thrive. I don't want a lot of questions coming up as to why the owner of Thrive and his girlfriend need security. While she's in the club one of you will keep watch outside and one of you will be posted by wherever she's working. If she's singing you will be in front of the stage with Jonah. If she's on the bar you will not be far from whichever bar she's stationed at. Are there any questions?"

"No, we've got it," Jake says, and Tony nods.

"We're leaving here in an hour to go car shopping. Can you two make sure we're not being followed?"

"Yes sir," Tony says. "We're going to head downstairs to check out the lobby and around the property. I want to know about all the entrances and exits. You have my cell number. Text me when you're ready to leave and we'll meet you in the garage."

"Excellent."

***

Skyler

The two guards walk out the door and Logan closes it, locking it behind them, and looks at me. His eyes scream dominance and for the first time I fear what is coming next. He smiles. "Nervous?"

"Well, the look on your face is saying you're about to take charge, and I guess since I'm not sure what you're going to take charge *of,* I'm a bit nervous, yes."

He bursts out laughing. "You really have no idea why I have this look on my face, miss 'I want to show off my ass'?"

I walk toward him. "I was only wearing them for you, sweetie."

"Then I guess you won't mind when I rip them off of you and slap that ass for teasing me. I had to stand behind the snack bar just now so I wouldn't show off the hard on I'm sporting."

A giggle escapes me. "I'm sorry, Logan. I didn't mean for that to happen." I give him my sweetest smile and his mask slips a little, though he quickly recovers.

He walks over to the couch, beckoning me over with his index finger. When I get to him, he unbuttons my shorts and pushes them down my legs.

"I don't mind you wearing shorts, but that ass is mine and no one else will see it. Am I clear?"

He tears my shorts so they are no longer wearable. He turns me around and leans me over the couch. "You have earned ten smacks, and then I'm going to fuck you good, but you won't come. Do you understand me?"

When I nod he snaps, "Answer me."

"I understand."

"Good." The first slap hits the right side of me.

"One," I say.

The second one comes down on my skin.

"Two."

The next few are quick, then he takes a minute to rub my ass, squeezing and massaging it. His hand comes down again, and when it does his fingers slap my pussy and I nearly come.

"Six."

He bends down to kiss me then quickly slaps me again. "Sev—" again before I can even finish my count, "eight." The last two he purposely slaps me so his fingers are nailing my pussy; he knows it's going to make it hard for me not to come.

I hear him fumble with his pants and I don't dare move; I'm dripping wet and ready to explode. Without warning he slams his cock deep inside me and I instantly fight the buildup that he has created. He's pounding into me and it reminds me of my past relationships and how cold they were. He's fucking me hard and for his pleasure only.

"Oh yes, love. Your pussy feels so good."

"Logan, please. I need to come."

He grabs my hips and pulls me toward him so I'm meeting him thrust for thrust. "You won't come," and as he says it, I feel him empty himself inside me. I'm frustrated both sexual and emotionally, and as soon as he pulls out of me, I run up the stairs and straight to the bathroom.

I hear him yell, "Don't you dare rub one out either!"

I can hear him coming up the stairs as I go in search of another pair of shorts that are not as short as the others and I fall to the floor crying when I can't find any. All of my shorts are that short, which means I have to wear leggings when it's eighty-five degrees outside.

When he appears at the doorway he has a look of confusion on his face when he sees me. "Love, what is wrong? Did I spank you too hard?"

I shake my head. "All my shorts are too short, so now I have to wear pants and it is hot out. And to top it off I didn't even get to come, so now I have nothing to wear *and* I'm sexual frustrated."

"I'm sorry, love. I only wanted you to see how frustrated I was standing there in front of two men with a hard on."

"I didn't pick these clothes! They were picked for me, so that isn't fair."

He sinks to the floor beside me. "You're right. I'm sorry. I thought you were trying to be a tease because you know I love your ass. I wasn't thinking about the fact that they were bought for you and I was embarrassed I couldn't leave the snack bar, so I got even madder at the thought of you teasing me. How can I make it better?"

"You can take me to buy some shorts that I can wear without my ass hanging out."

"You got it. And I'll make the rest of up to you

later, I promise."

I stand from the floor and change my clothes so we can go out.

***

Logan

Seeing Sky on the floor crying nearly broke me. God, what was I thinking? I saw her in those shorts and freaking lost it. Now I need to make it up to her. She walks into the bathroom to wash her face and freshen up. I pick up the shorts and take them into the bathroom to her.

"Here, love. I want you to wear these. We'll go shopping after we pick out a new car for you."

She rewards me with the most beautiful smile. "Thank you for taking such good care of me."

"Today I didn't, but I'm going to fix that. Come on, I have a surprise for you."

"Can you tell me what it is?"

I chuckle. "I can tell you that I changed my mind about the kind of car I want to get you and I know where to go to get it."

Skyler is excited to see what I'm getting her and I'm thrilled to see her so happy after I messed up so badly. We climb into my rental car and head down the highway to the Porsche dealership. I need to get her a car that she'll look good in and I have decided that a Boxster is the car for her. I may get her something a bit bigger later, but for now she deserves something fun. She's fidgeting in the seat on the side of me, and I can't help but wonder what's going through that beautiful mind of hers.

"What's up, love?"

"I'm not good with surprises. I'm anxious to see where you're taking me."

"I'm taking you to buy a car that you're going to look magnificent driving. Did you like my convertible before it got all messed up?"

She gives me a sideways grin. "I loved your convertible. You can almost always drive with the top down here!"

I pull into the local Porsche dealership.

"Holy shit. You're buying me a Porsche?"

"To be more specific, I'm buying you a Boxster. Red with black top and all the top notch gadgets inside."

"Thank you, Logan. Isn't that a bit much, though? I mean, you can buy me an Audi or a BMW if you want me to have something nicer, but a Porsche?"

A salesman walks up to us. He shakes my hand and says, "Hello, I'm Joe. What can I do for you today?"

"I'm Logan Michaels, and this is my girlfriend Skyler. I would like to buy her a Boxster. Do you have any available in the deep red on the lot?"

"I certainly do. Follow me, please."

Skyler and I walk hand in hand behind him.

"I want it fully loaded," I say to the guy's back as we are walking toward the car I want for her.

"Oh my god, Logan. It's gorgeous," Skyler gushes when we reach it.

"I knew you would like it."

"Sweetie, this is only a two-seater. What if I

want to go out with my friends? We won't fit in my car."

"You guys mainly hang at Thrive," I say with a shrug. "If you want to go somewhere else you can either use my car or I'll buy you a bigger one later."

"Wait," the salesman says with sudden recognition. "You're *the* Logan Michaels? Like, son of the actress and owner of Thrive?"

"Yes, Joe, I'm that Logan Michaels," I say with a chuckle. "Now, is this fully loaded?"

"Yes, sir. It's the only Boxster I have that is. We had one in black but sold it last week."

"We'll take it."

We follow him in to fill out paperwork, and thirty minutes later the security team is there to drive the rental back and we take my new car out for a spin.

"Logan, you can drive it. I'm going to be nervous as hell driving this."

"You need to drive it at some point. It's your car."

"And you spent ninety thousand dollars on it. I don't want to dent it."

I kiss her gently. "You're not going to dent it. And if you do, we have great insurance that will replace it, so there is nothing to worry about."

She takes a deep breath and climbs into the driver's seat.

"Head to Rodeo Drive. We'll go shopping for some clothes for you. We should probably look for some dresses for Club Temptation too."

I direct her on where to go, and she follows my directions perfectly. A few minutes later she's parking the car in a safe garage, and we head out to do some shopping. While we walk down the strip, Skyler looks into windows and I know she's paranoid about spending more money, so I pull her into a store to look around. When she finds some shorts and capris she likes I tell the girl behind the counter to get her whatever she wants.

"What can I help you with today?" she asks Skyler. They talk back and forth while I sit and watch her try on a few things.

The girl comes back over to me. "She'll be right out. She picked one pair of shorts and one pair of capris. She's changing and then she'll be right out."

I smile at her. "Please give me four pairs of each in her size and feel free to pick a few different colors if you have them."

"Yes sir." She walks off to do as I have asked.

When Skyler comes out of the changing room, I have a bag in my hand with her clothes all taken care of.

"Thank you, sweetie. I think you'll like the shorts I chose much better." She kisses me and we walk out the door. Tony is outside waiting to collect the bag before he heads off into the opposite direction as us.

"I was thinking we could have lunch at Pacific Seafood Grill up the street. The food is delicious and they have outdoor seating so we can enjoy the magnificent weather."

"That sounds perfect."

***

Skyler

My phone rings as I walk into the house.

"Hello, Miss Sadie!" I answer. "What's up?"

"I just got done looking at that venue that has the gorgeous trees and flowers outside. Do you remember?"

"Yeah, that was one of the two in your budget, right?"

"Yeah, it's perfect. We booked it on the spot!"

"That's great! I'm so happy for you guys." I cover the phone and look at Logan, who'd followed me in carrying my bags. "Sadie and Jonah booked the venue for the wedding." He nods and walks away with my bags.

"What are you doing?" Sadie asks.

"I'm walking in the door with Logan. He took me shopping today."

"Oh, that is cool. What did he buy you?"

I purposely say it casually because I know she's going to freak. "A pair of shorts, a Porsche, a pair of capris, some—"

"He bought you a fucking Porsche!" she screams into the phone.

Logan laughs as he comes back downstairs seeing me pull the phone away from my ear and he can hear her scream.

"And some dresses for formal events or when I sing."

"I can't believe he bought you a Porsche."

"Me neither. Hey, are you guys coming over for dinner on Monday again so we can start our weekly ritual?"

175

"Of course we are. I need to show you the pics I took of the hall."

"Great! And I want to show you my new car!"

"You're so lucky!" she whines in my ear.

"Listen, I have to go because Logan is waiting for me, and I'm not sure what our plans are for the rest of the day but I'll see you Monday for sure!"

"Later, Skyler!"

I end the call, and when I turn around Logan is leaning against the snack bar with a beer in his hand. "So what should we do for the rest of the day?"

"How about a bath to wash off this sweat from walking around outside?"

"That sounds like a plan. We can order some takeout when we're done." He takes a sip of his beer. "Would you like some wine to take up with you?"

"Sure, I would love a glass of wine. I'll go start the tub while you get the wine."

"See you upstairs in a minute," he says.

I run up the stairs. I want to take my panties off before he rips them because I like this pair. I rush into the bathroom, start the tub, and while I'm hurrying up to strip he comes in and cracks up laughing.

"What are you doing, Skyler?"

Damn, I wasn't quick enough. "I really like these panties so I was trying to hurry up and get them off so you wouldn't rip them."

"I'll buy you a hundred pairs if you like those, so you won't have to worry about it."

"That is such a waste of money. And panties.

You need to gain some control over ripping them off of me."

Logan kisses me softly, promising to try. "Can we ditch the bath for a second?"

"I want to make love to you in the tub." I pull his polo shirt over his head, exposing his chest. I lean up on my toes to kiss him, unbutton his pants, and kiss my way down his neck, pulling him toward the tub.

He kicks his shoes off and finishes removing his pants while I climb into the tub. The water is welcoming and I can't wait to ride him as soon as he's in. He walks to the edge of the tub with his massive erection pointing up to his stomach. I start at his shaft and lick all the way up to his tip, to a small drop of precum. He groans, and I take him deep in my mouth but don't let him stay long. Backing away from the edge of the tub, I tell him, "Sit."

He has given me control and it's killing him, but I love it. He does as he's told.

"Good boy. Now I'm going to ride you like you've never been ridden. You're not in charge tonight, I am. I'll decide when I come. Am I clear?" He nods. "Good."

I slowly sink down onto his shaft and as I do, his hips slide up to meet me. I move my hips up and down. Logan presses me down further as his hips grind into me.

"Stop!" I turn around so my back is to his front. I slip him back inside me and place my hands on the edge of the tub, leaning slightly forward and grind my hips while he's buried deep inside me. His hips are moving with mine, he's groaning, and I can feel his legs tighten under me as he fights off his release.

"Love, I'm not going to last much longer like this."

"Don't come yet. I'm not ready." I start riding him harder and harder.

"Come on, Sky, give it to me." He sounds pained.

"Not yet." He reaches around to play with my clit as I slam down on his lap. "Now!" I shout, and just like that we are both coming together.

"Logan, that was awesome."

"You were right about one thing. You definitely rode me like I've never been ridden before. That was amazing."

I collapse against him.

He kisses the top of my head and says, "I love you, Skyler."

Without even thinking I reply, "I love you too, Logan."

Chapter 13

Skyler

I park my Porsche and walk up to the back entrance of Club Temptation. I have my dress in hand and Tony is right behind me. Jake is in the club checking things out. Mikey left me a spot right under the cameras so if anything happens to my new car it will be on tape. I knock on the back door and a huge guy opens it.

"Hi, I'm Skyler. I'm singing here tonight."

He nods toward Tony. "Who's he?"

"He's my security. I have two guys. One is already inside checking things out." He nods and pushes the door open further for us to walk in.

"Hey, Sky!" Mikey shouts. "I thought I heard that beautiful voice of yours."

I smile at him and give him a hug. "Hey, Mikey. How's it going?"

"All is good, my friend. Follow me and I'll show you where you can change and then we'll do a mic check. The doors open shortly."

179

"That sounds good to me! By the way, this is Tony, my other security guard. Jake is already here and I assume you met him."

"Yeah. Logan is worried, huh?"

"Yes. The creep showed up at a diner I was at and was chillin' on my car. It was pretty freaky he knew I was there."

"I'm sorry you're dealing with that. Well listen, you only sing until about 11:00, and then we switch over to a DJ so you don't have to sing all night. Come see me before you leave, okay?"

"Sure."

"This is your changing room. Go ahead and get dressed, and then I'll meet you out at the stage for a sound check and confirm the list I want you to sing."

"Sure. See you in a few." I head in to change. It's a small room with a little vanity that has a mirror with lights so I can check my makeup. I set my bag down on the side of the vanity and hang my dress on the rack, then take off the clothes I'm wearing. I slip on my sexy black dress and bold red heels, check my hair in the mirror one last time, and open the door to find Tony standing there waiting for me.

"All set?" he asks.

"Let's do this."

We head to the front of the club where we spot the stage. Mikey is already there getting things together. He whistles at me. "Damn girl, you look fantastic!"

"Thanks, Mikey. Do you have that song list for me?"

He hands it to me. "I'm going to be honest," he says. "There aren't too many people here during the two hours you're singing, but my hope is to get people in here earlier with the live entertainment before we start to jam with club music."

"I have no problem with anything on this list." I take the mic and start my sound check.

"Mikey, the feedback is too loud."

"I can hear it. Hold on one second." He runs into the booth, presses some buttons, and tells me to try again.

I wink and give him thumbs up. "Can I get water with lemon for the stage? I can't let my throat get dry."

"Sure thing. And listen, if you need to take a break, take one. Just let the crowd know you'll be back in five and it's cool. Okay?"

"You got it."

The club is open and I'm on stage doing my thing. Although I'm nervous that Billy is going to show or I'm going to screw something up, I'm genuinely enjoying myself. As Mikey said, the crowd is not large, but they appear to be enjoying my singing, clapping and hooting when as I finish songs. I'm about halfway through my night when I need a break.

"Thank you, ladies and gentlemen. I'm going to take a quick five minute break and I'll be back with you."

I walk off the stage and Tony is right there. "Are you okay?" he questions, concerned.

"Yes. I need the bathroom and more water."

He follows me to the ladies room so I can take

181

care of business. On the way I hear him calling to Jake, "Make sure Sky has water with lemon at the stage when we get back. She only has five minutes."

I arrive back at the stage and Mikey is waiting. "Girl, you can sing. You're doing a great job!"

I take a sip of my water. "Thanks, Mikey. I'm enjoying myself. Thank you for letting me sing at your club."

"The pleasure is all mine."

I climb back up on stage. "Okay, who's ready for some more music?" I laugh when I get a bunch of screams from the audience. "Okay, okay, here we go." I begin the second half of my song list.

After I have completed the set, I head into the back room to change my clothes. When I come out, the DJ is playing and the club is starting to pick up a little. Mikey is on the dance floor and I head over to join him. He asks me to dance with him. I'm dancing and having a good time while my security team is talking to each other as they take positions that will allow them to keep me safe.

***

Logan

"Hey, Shane, can you handle the club for a little bit? I want to surprise Skyler at Club Temptation."

"Sure, Logan, no problem."

"I'll let Jonah know I'm leaving and I'll be back in a little bit."

"Cool. Have fun!" he yells, running to get liquor

for one of the bars.

"Hey, Jonah," I say into the ear wig, "I'm heading to the club to surprise Skyler. I'll be back. I talked to Shane as well, and he said he's got everything under control."

"No problem. See you in a bit!"

I get in my car so excited to see my girl sing. I have a huge smile on my face as I'm driving over to the club. I love my girl and I really love to hear her sing. It almost killed me to be at Thrive for as long as I have, but I needed to get some stuff done. I hope I don't miss her. I'm not sure how long Mikey has her on stage tonight because I know he has a DJ too.

I pull up to the club and practically run to the door. I give them my name and am instantly let into the club, then am totally disappointed when I hear the DJ playing and not my girl's voice on stage. I'm bummed I wasn't here to support her. My eyes are roaming the club because I'm trying to figure out where she is, and that's when I spot her. What the fuck?

I push my way to the dance floor to find her dancing with Mikey. I grab her arm, spinning her around. "What the fuck, Skyler?"

"Logan, what's your problem?"

"What's my problem? I come here to surprise you and catch you dancing with my boy, and you want to know why I'm mad?"

"You need to stop. I got off stage a few minutes ago, and Mikey asked me to dance a few songs with him before we talked about my next gig."

I yank her arm and pull her toward the door. She

snatches her arm away from me. "Let go of me. You're embarrassing me *and* your friend. Who the hell do you think you are?"

"I'm your fucking boyfriend, and you're coming with me."

"The fuck I am. You need to calm the hell down, and when you do, call me."

My jaw drops because I can't believe she said that to me and then walked away. I don't even know where she went, but Tony and Jake have followed her so at least I know she's safe.

Mikey comes up to me. "You're lucky you're my boy or I would punch you in the face right now. Come with me." He pulls me into his office, slamming the door shut. "What the fuck is your problem?"

"I don't know, I freaked out when I saw her with you."

"Logan, I know Lindsey did a number on you, but you better figure your shit out because Skyler is for real and you may have lost her over your jealous bullshit."

"Fuck, Mikey. What the hell am I going to do?"

"If I were you, I would let her cool down and then beg for forgiveness. Have you told her about Lindsey?"

"No."

"Looks like you will be, because explaining that shit may be the only thing to save your sorry ass."

I yank at my hair in frustration. "Mikey, man, I'm so sorry."

"Listen, I get it and you're my boy. Don't sweat it, but don't do it again either. Yeah I was dancing with your girl, but I would never disrespect you by pulling what Nate did. Got it?"

"Yeah, I got it. Listen, I need to go make some calls."

I walk out to my car, and the first person I call is Jonah. "Hey, have you heard from Skyler?"

"No, but Sadie called and said Skyler is sleeping at our house tonight. What the fuck did you do?"

"I fucked up, and now I have to figure out how to fix it. I'm on my way back to the club now."

I cut the call and drive straight back to the club.

***

Skyler

I need to slow down or I'm going to get myself killed. I'm so upset I don't even care right now. I can't believe Logan did that to me in a club that I'm trying to build my name in. I'll never be able to sing there again because I'm now known as the singer with the jealous boyfriend. It isn't like I was dancing with some random guy either; it was one of his good friends. I seriously have no idea what his problem is.

I slow down to take the exit from the freeway and hit a red light. I take a deep breath, trying to keep my tears at bay. He can't tell me he loves me one minute, then not trust me the next. That doesn't work.

I stomp on the gas as soon as the light turns green, and because I'm upset, I don't see the cop hiding around the corner. He immediately pulls me over. I punch my brand new twenty thousand dollar steering wheel, pissed because if I wasn't driving this fucking Porsche I probably wouldn't have been pulled over.

Please be John, please be John, I think to myself as I wait for him to approach.

The officer taps on the window and I roll it down. It isn't John. I automatically hand over my license and registration.

"Going a bit fast tonight, aren't you?"

"Sorry, officer, I had a fight with my boyfriend and I was upset."

"I can see that, but it doesn't give you the right to drive crazy. You'll get over a broken heart, but you may not get over your injuries if you smash this car."

"I'm sorry. I'll slow down. I'm right up the street from my friend's house where I'm spending the night."

"I'll be right back," he says, walking away from my car to run my plate and make sure the car is mine. While I wait for what feels like an eternity, I send Sadie a text.

Skyler: *Got pulled over for speeding. Be there in a few.*

Sadie: *Slow down and get here safe.*

The cop walks back to my car and hands me a ticket, my license, and registration and tells me to have a great night.

I roll up my window. Wonderful. I fought with

186

my boyfriend and now I have a seventy-five dollar ticket. Thank God he didn't catch me on the freeway.

I pull up to Sadie's, and as soon as I ring her buzzer she lets me in. I go running up the stairs and she's waiting with a hug for me.

I burst into tears. "I can't believe him. He was like a raging lunatic, and it was so embarrassing."

"Aww, sweetie, it's okay," she says, rubbing my back to soothe me. She hands me a tissue and a glass of wine she has already poured and pulls me toward the couch. "Tell me what happened."

"I went to the club to sing like I was supposed to. When I was done, Mikey asked me to find him so we could talk about my next gig with him. He was on the dance floor with some friends so he asked me to join him. I was off the clock and figured it was no big deal." I dab my eyes and take a deep breath. "All of a sudden I feel someone yank on my arm and when I turn around it's Logan, livid that I'm dancing with Mikey. He screams at me, 'What the fuck are you doing? You're coming with me!' That's when I told him the hell I was, that he needed to calm down and call me when he did."

I take a sip of my wine. "That's when I got my stuff and called you. I do not want to go back there. I don't even know how I'm going to face him at work tomorrow. I don't want to be unprofessional and call out sick because that will make it worse."

"I agree. You need to go to work so you can show him that you two can work together, not to mention you don't want other people at the club to start thinking every time you two fight you'll

187

disappear."

"Would you mind going shopping with me tomorrow so I can get an outfit for work? I don't want to go to the house unless he has called me much calmer to talk things over."

"Me? Have a problem shopping? Come on, girl, really? Of course I'll go shopping with you. I also think you should call him though. I know he screwed up, but I do believe he loves you."

I shake my head. "He screwed up, so *he* should be calling *me*."

"I partially agree with that, but this is a relationship, and if you love him, give him the chance to explain."

I finish off my wine and ask if she has more. I want to get drunk and not think about it tonight. I'm disappointed because for the first time in my life I allowed someone in and didn't screw up. Yet here I sit on my best friend's couch, heartbroken and not knowing what Logan is doing or how he's feeling.

Chapter 14

Logan

I sit in my home office trying to work on ideas for a new club, and I realize the only thing I'm doing is trying to block Skyler from my mind. Why, I don't know. I love her, I know I do, but I don't know how to fix what I've done. I've been debating texting her all night, but Mikey said I needed to let her cool down, and I'm not sure how long that takes.

I don't even know what to do about work tonight. I keep playing over in my head the events of last night and what Jonah said to me when I got back: *"Dude, you fucked this up. You need to fix it. For the first time she has let someone in and you hurt her."* He even told me Sadie texted him that she was at their house a mess over what I did. My phone pings and I check it; it's a text from Jonah.

Jonah: Skyler plans on working tonight, what are you going to do?

Logan: Fuck! I figured she would call out.

Jonah: Nope wants to prove to everyone that she won't run because you two had a fight. She's even going shopping for clothes so she'll have something to wear.

I pick up the phone and call Tony. "Hey, man, Skyler is leaving her friend Sadie's to go shopping. Make sure to keep your distance but follow her."
"You got it."

Logan: Sky hates shopping.

Jonah: I know.

Logan: How do I fix this?

Jonah: The hell if I know. I think you need to start by figuring out why you were so mad and then talking to her about it.

I take a deep breath while I try to figure out how to respond. I know why I freaked. Can I tell her what happened with Lindsey? And will it make it worse that I basically compared her to my ex without even meaning to?

Logan: I'll talk to her tonight.

Jonah: Don't piss her off before her shift. We don't need her running out tonight.

Logan: Good point. Talk to you later.

I text her next to see if we can talk tonight after our shift. I need to fix things with her or it's going to be a long healing process. It has only been one night and I'm exhausted because I couldn't sleep without her in my bed.

Logan: Can we talk after work tonight?

Her response is immediate.

Skyler: I don't know. Heading out with Sadie right now to drop off the Porsche and pick up my car.

Logan: That is your car. Please don't do this. I know I fucked up and I want to fix it.

Skyler: Well texting me isn't going to fix it and I don't want the car. I'm not with you for your money, I was with you because I love you and I thought you loved me.

Logan: I do love you, which is why I want to apologize and fix this.

Skyler: I'm not sure how you plan on fixing this but trust is a deal breaker. Figure out whether you trust me or not and call me when you do.

She's right. I have to trust her, and I thought I

did right up until I saw her dancing with Mikey. I try to shake it off and go back to looking at more locations for another club. At least if I open another club, I can work out of the other one while I figure things out with Skyler.

My agent sends me three different locations to look at for potential clubs. One is a club that is struggling and looking to be taken over, and the other two are abandoned buildings that would need to be constructed into clubs and given new identities and need a lot of promoting. I email the agent and tell her I want to see all three as soon as possible.

The good thing is I can work on all of this stuff from outside of the club, so if I need to stay out of the club for the night I can and then see her tomorrow, or maybe she'll come over with Jonah and Sadie for dinner on Monday.

My email pings and it's the agent.

Can show you the abandoned ones whenever you want and I'll work on an appointment for the other one.

I send her a message back telling her to meet me at the first one in one hour.

I run upstairs and quickly shower and dress. I'm out the door in thirty minutes and on my way to the first location. While I drive there, I tell myself this is what I need, a project to work on so I can clear my head. I know Sky loves me and isn't Lindsey. Now I have to figure out how to stop myself from overreacting. Maybe if I tell her what happened she'll understand and we can move past this. I turn

192

up the radio, and I instantly think of Skyler and her singing, so I shut it off. A few minutes later I pull up to the first location. I jump out of the car when I see Ally waiting for me by the door. She punches in the code number on the lock box so she can pull out the key.

"Hey, Logan, good to see you!"

"Hey, Ally, good to see you too."

"Is the club doing that well you're ready to buy again already? I didn't think we would be doing this for about two years."

"The club is doing amazingly well, and if I want to be ready to expand, I need to start looking. It took me a while to find the perfect location last time."

"Yeah, it can be hard sometimes. This one isn't in the best location, but the area is on the rise, and a good club could be what it needs to help push it along."

"I'm not too sure I'm happy about this location. It's in the middle of nowhere."

"There are ups and downs to that, and you know that as well as I do."

I walk into the building. It's a good thing it's daylight or you wouldn't be able to see a thing in here. There is no electricity and the place is one big empty room. I walk through looking around to see if the place would work, and to be honest it isn't a bad set up. I could make the VIP rooms up above like at Thrive to give them a connected feel but probably only have room for one bar as opposed to two. There could be a small catwalk for the ladies opposite the VIP section which would give the guys a show.

"Okay, I've seen enough. Let's move to the next location." I get into my car and head in the direction of the next building. I pull up and wait for Ally because I left without her. I know I'm being a dick, but I'm in a shitty mood. There's only one person who can improve my mood and she won't talk to me.

Ally pulls up, and I get out of my car to follow her to the entrance. She unlocks it, and it's worse than the first one. "Come on, Ally, this place is a piece of shit."

"It's in a great location and you can expand on it. There is plenty of room around it."

"If I'm going to expand, I might as well knock the thing down and start over. There is no room to do anything here. Call me when you find something for real or when you get me an appointment to check out that other club."

I shake my head and walk out. I head to the florist to send Skyler some flowers before she gets to work tonight. When I pull in, I ask the girl if she can deliver two dozen red roses to Jonah's address by 5:30. I pay for the flowers and pick a card to write her a note.

Skyler,

I'm sorry I was a fool! I do trust you and want to be with you. Please help me figure this out.

Love,

Logan

I hand the woman the card, and she shakes her head. "I see more apologies written on these little cards than you can imagine. If you want to fix things take the flowers to her yourself. Don't have them delivered. You need to talk to her."

"Why does everyone keep saying that to me? I want to talk to her. She's the one who said she isn't sure if she's ready yet."

"If you deliver them, she has no choice but to listen, right?"

I shake my head. "Who am I kidding? She isn't going to care if I have flowers delivered. I bought her a damn Porsche that she dropped back off at my house. What the hell are flowers going to do?"

"Baby, want to start out fresh? You can buy *me* a Porsche."

I laugh at her bluntness.

"I'll deliver your flowers," she says, "but you're right, they're not going to fix your problem. I'm willing to bet you know what you have to do, so how about you do it and get your girl back? If she's willing to give back a Porsche, I bet she's worth keeping around."

"You have no idea."

***

Skyler

"I can't believe you're giving up the Porsche. Why don't you drive it? You know you want to," Sadie whines.

"Because maybe he'll realize that I'm not with

him for his money or whatever his issue is, and we'll be able to get past this problem. If I continue to drive it, then it looks like I only wanted him for his money and that's not the case."

I pull up to the valet and ask him to bring my Honda around. He looks at me like I have ten heads and says, "Yes, ma'am."

"Miss Jones!" Greg calls.

"Yes?"

"I'm sorry, I don't mean to intrude, but I overheard Mr. Michaels talking last night about your situation and, well, I want you to know he's a good man. He has lived here a long time and has been through a lot. You have made a very positive impact in his life. I hope you two can work it out."

"That's sweet, Greg, thank you. I hope we can work it out too."

"I'm sorry if I overstepped. I don't usually get involved. I wanted you to know he was a bit of a mess both last night and when I saw him leave earlier today."

"Do you have any idea where he went?"

"No, he just called down for his car and took off."

The valet comes around with my Honda.

"Thank you for the information, Greg. I'm sure we'll work things out."

He nods and heads back to his spot at the door, smiling. He knows exactly what I'm doing. Sadie and I climb into my car and head off to shop. Since I don't have Logan's money and refuse to go back to the expensive ass stores on Rodeo Drive, we head over to the Fashion District to do a little shopping and grab some lunch.

"Shop first then lunch!" Sadie says as I pull up and park.

I find a pair of skinny jeans, and I need a top and some boots to wear for tonight.

Sadie pulls me into one of the stores. "There is a super cute gray top over there that would look great on you and then you can buy black boots."

"That's cute. It's off the shoulder though, so I'll have to get a tank top to put under it." I find it in a medium and head over to a table where they have a bunch of tank tops, and I choose one in black. "Now to find some boots."

Sadie links her arm through mine, and we head off to the shoe store.

"Do you think he's as miserable as I am?" I ask my best friend. "I'm having fun with you but I'm dying on the inside."

She smiles and shakes her head. "I'm pretty confident he's as miserable as you are and probably out doing the same thing you are, and that's trying to figure out what to do."

I try to hold my tears back and I'm struggling. My fun lasted for all of thirty minutes.

Sadie and I walk into the shoe store. I find a pair of boots, but I'm no longer as excited because I can't help but wonder what Logan is doing.

We head to get some lunch, and as soon as we sit down my phone pings.

Logan: I can't even listen to music without thinking about you.

197

A tear slides down my cheek.

"What's wrong, Sky?" Sadie asks.

I show her my phone. "I need him, but he also needs to know he hurt me. He can't do this to me ever again because if he does I'm done. I need him to trust me and if he can't then we have no relationship."

Skyler: I'm thinking about you too :-(

Logan: Will you come home and talk to me tonight?

Skyler: I don't know. Have you decided if you trust me or not?

Logan: You'll see as soon as you get to Sadie's.

I smile and wonder what he did.

"You went from sad to smiling real quick."

"He asked me to come home and talk tonight, and I asked him if he decided if he could trust me and his response was, 'You'll see when you get back to Sadie's place.' Now I want to get back to see what he did."

She bursts out laughing. "You need to eat before work, and at this point you'll have enough time to eat and then shower before you have to head to work. Our lunch has turned into more of an early dinner."

"You're right. I haven't eaten all day." We are at a little cafe and the menu options are perfect because they are quick, filling options and I'll be able to get back to Sadie's to see what Logan did. Jonah is home so I'm wondering if he helped him pull something off. I'm bouncing my leg under the table from the suspense. Anxious to see Logan, I eat quickly.

"Girl, if you don't stop fidgeting, you're going to knock this entire table over."

"I'm sorry. I told Logan I don't like surprises, and now I have no idea what he's up to."

"Okay, okay, let's get out of here so you can find out what's going on."

I laugh because I know it's killing her too. As we leave, her phone pings and she grins. "It's Jonah," she says as she replies to his text.

We walk the short distance back to my car. We put my bags in the back seat and we both climb in. My phone pings next.

Logan: Where are you?

Skyler: Leaving the fashion district why?

Logan: Just curious xoxo.

"He's up to no good!" I say as I drive off toward Sadie's house.

"Why do you say that?" Sadie asks, and even her voice sounds suspicious now.

"Because first Jonah texts you and then Logan texts me. That doesn't seem suspicious to you?"

She shrugs and stares straight ahead.

***

Logan

The florist is right; actions speak louder than words, and flowers with a cheesy apology won't mean shit to Skyler. It's time to go big or go home alone. I text Jonah.

Logan: Hey, can I recruit your help?

Jonah: Is it to get Skyler back?

Logan: Of course.

Jonah: Then I'm in! How can I help?

Logan: I need to use your house since they are going back there. I'll be there soon. I have to make a quick stop.

Jonah: See you soon.

I head to a jewelry store to pick out a ring for Skyler. When I walk in, I tell the jeweler exactly what I want. He shows me what he has; I pick one out, pay for it, and run out the door. I have to be quick because I know Skyler won't be gone long. My next stop is back to the florist. I walk in, and the same woman is behind the counter.

"So you were right," I say. "I need to change my order and I'll take the original two dozen with me. I need loose rose petals too. Can you do that?"

"Absolutely. What are you planning, if you don't mind me asking?" she asks, full of excitement.

"I bought a promise ring, and I want rose petals going up the stairs, and then I'll have the two dozen roses for her when I give her the ring. Do you think that's better?"

"As long as you explain yourself, I think it'll be perfect. It's definitely better than sending her flowers." She heads out back to get the rose petals, and when she comes back she hands me my two dozen roses along with petals. "The petals are on me. Good luck, sweetie."

I grin widely. "I promise you much more business in the future."

She laughs as I head toward the door. "Go get your girl!"

I run out feeling much better about what I'm doing. I race over to Jonah's house and park up the street so Skyler won't spot my car. I run to the house and ring the buzzer.

Jonah buzzes me in. As soon as he opens the door, he says, "Hurry. I texted Sadie a second ago. They're on their way."

I send Skyler a quick text.

Logan: Where are you?

She responds pretty quickly.

Skyler: Leaving the fashion district, why?

Logan: Just curious xoxo.

I spread the rose petals out all over Jonah's hallway floor with a promise to clean it up later and continue into the house, where I plan to wait on my knees begging her to forgive me. Jonah's phone pings, and it's Sadie saying they are pulling up now.

"Logan, they're here. Are you ready to grovel?"

"Shut up. She's worth it!"

"I know, and if it was Sadie I would do the same thing."

He fist bumps me, and I get down on my knees with the ring in one hand and roses in the other. When the girls walk through the door, Skyler's jaw drops.

"What are you doing?"

"Skyler, I know I messed up so bad, but I'm on my knees begging you to forgive me. I love you so much. I have a ring I would be honored if you'd wear as a symbol of my vow to never mistrust you again and to promise you that someday I will make you my wife. If you'll come home with me tonight, I also promise to explain my actions and start spending the rest of my life making it up to you."

"You didn't need to buy me a ring to say you were sorry. The words spoke volumes. Yes, I'll go home with you and hear you out, but know, and I mean this with all my heart, if you ever do that to me again we're done. I was devastated and embarrassed, and I never want to go through that again. However, I love you enough to give you another chance."

I jump up off my knees and embrace her into the biggest hug, pulling away only to kiss her. "God, woman, I was only without you for one night and I'm a fucking mess. Trust me, I'll never piss you off again."

Skyler chuckles. "I doubt that's true, but we'll see."

Anybody who worked last night knew I fucked up, and as soon as we walk into the club I can see they're all on edge, gauging my mood.

"Good evening, everyone," I say as we walk in so they'll relax a little.

Skyler grins. "Did you scare them last night?"

"Yeah, I think so. They won't have to worry though, because as long as you're coming home with me, all will be good. I love you, Skyler."

"I love you too, Logan. I have to get to work now so my boss doesn't fire me."

I laugh and walk away to prepare for the club to open.

***

It's already 1:30, and my team should be finished with last call since we close at 2:00. The club's been packed all night, and my incredible team has everything running smoothly as usual. I'm sitting in my office watching everything unfold from the cameras. I could open a new club if I wanted to. This team could totally manage this place while I bounced between two clubs. I think I want to take Skyler away for a couple of days first, though. A quick impromptu vacation. Where should we go is the question. Maybe I'll ask her tonight if there's somewhere special she'd like to go for a few days. We could go Sunday to Tuesday and not miss any time from work.

Right now it's time for me to head out and get

this place closed up, because unfortunately I still have to explain my actions to her and hope she'll stay with me after I explain what happened with Lindsay.

***

Skyler

"Your ring is stunning," Kelly says as we are cleaning up our bar.

"Thanks! It's a promise ring from Logan."

"Aww, that is sweet!"

All I've been able to think about tonight is how much I can't wait to get home to hear what he has to say. If I even remotely slowed down, I started thinking about it.

Logan comes out as Kelly and I are done cleaning up our bar and about to head to bar one to help them stock and finish cleaning up from last call.

"Nice job getting things cleaned up, ladies," Logan says. "What do you have left to do?"

"Just stock and help clean up bar one," I reply.

Logan looks nervous, and it makes me smile. Although I feel slightly bad, let's be real; he made me feel pretty shitty last night and it wasn't fair. If he thinks he can buy me a ring and all is fine, he's crazy. He'll be spilling his guts tonight, and then I'll decide if we're good or not. He walks away to check on the other bar, and Kelly and I head to the back to get what we need. We carry it out to bar one while they're washing glasses and putting them away.

"Hey, Skyler, Shane is going to close up so we can get out of here," Logan asks. "Are you ready?"

"We haven't finished cleaning up yet," I throw out there, not wanting the team to get mad I'm leaving early because I'm the boss' girlfriend.

"We're good, Sky," Shane says and then Kelly jumps in too.

"Yeah, we're almost done. Go on and get out of here."

I raise both my brows at them. "Are you guys sure? Don't cover because I'm his girlfriend. I'll carry my own weight."

"Seriously, go," Shane says. "It's fine! You can cover one of us another night."

"Okay, cool. Have a good night." I hug each of my friends and walk out with Logan.

We get into his rental car and we're both quiet. There's a lot of tension in the air.

"When are you going to get a car?" I ask.

He shrugs. "I don't know. I have more important things to take care of right now. I'm hoping to go on Monday if you and I are good."

I chuckle to myself then turn to look out the window again.

A short while later, he pulls up to his place and I climb out of the car to see Greg standing there.

"Good evening, Miss Jones. Good to see you."

"Good to see you too. Greg, do you ever sleep?"

He bursts out laughing. "Yes, ma'am, I do. The night doorman called out sick so I agreed to stay."

"You're a good man, Greg." Only he and I know I'm referring to our conversation from earlier. I walk to the elevator and press the button while I wait for Logan.

He walks up behind me and asks, "What was that all about with Greg?"

"I just happen to notice that he's always here, so I asked him if he ever sleeps. He told me the other doorman called out so he offered to stay."

The elevator comes and we ride it up to his floor. We walk into his place and he offers me a glass of wine, which I eagerly accept, hoping it'll calm my nerves a little. I have to admit I'm a bit nervous because *he* is so nervous.

"So…I guess we should talk," he says, handing me a glass of white wine.

"Yeah, we probably should, because no matter your reasoning it's important you understand how I felt in that moment and even after."

"I know nothing excuses my behavior, and I've already apologized to Mikey. Luckily for me, he knows about my history with my ex and why I reacted the way I did. He told me if he hadn't known me better he would have punched me in the face for what I did to you."

"Wow. He's a good guy. I can tell and I've only known him a short time."

"I know, and I'm lucky to have him as a friend." He takes a deep breath. "I was once in love with this girl Lindsay. We were together for almost five years. We were even engaged to be married. She knew I had jealousy issues and she used them against me once she knew I was in love with her. I gave her the world, Skyler, and I would have done anything for her until I caught her fucking my best friend. When I walked in on them, I stood there and watched, not knowing what to do. I felt foolish for not seeing it sooner. I was devastated, and I vowed from that day forward no woman would hurt me that way ever again. I spent a long time focused on building up the club I worked in and tried dating other women but never felt like I could trust them. Until I met you. You were sweet and shy and your smile lit up my life. When I saw you dancing with Mikey, my insecurities came back to haunt me and I lost it. I'm so sorry, Skyler. I'm sure it'll take some time for you to forgive me, but please try. I do truly love you and promise I'll never behave like that again."

"Like I told you at Sadie's, what you did was embarrassing and hurtful, but I love you, Logan, and I want a life with you. I'll forgive you this once. I know I told you in the past I would sabotage my relationships to leave men, so I can understand why you reacted the way you did. Let me be clear, though; my relationships did not compare to what you and I have, and I will not do to you what I did to them. Going forward we talk, because this is the only free pass I'll give you."

He pulls me in for a kiss. "Thank you, Skyler. Now I have one question for you."

"What, sweetie?"

"If I were to tell you that I want to take you away for three or four days, where would you want to go?"

"Hmmm, I've never thought about it. Can I have some time to think about it?"

"Yes. I want to take you away for a few days of

some quiet time, just the two of us."

Chapter 15

Skyler

The last two weeks have been absolutely delightful. We've continued to get together with Sadie and Jonah on Monday nights, and next week we're adding Shane and Katie to the mix because they've been seeing each other since I introduced them a few weeks ago. I'm happy for them and hope it works out.

It has been a quiet week as far as my stalker goes. Logan called for an update, and all they could tell us is that the guy is laying low and they don't know where. They found the bat that matched the damage to Logan's car so it was definitely him who beat the crap out of it. Logan still thinks Troy played a part in it, especially since we found out he and Billy were in rehab together, and also because Troy was so pissed that Logan refused to drop the charges. Billy admitted to getting a few texts from Troy, attempting to bribe him, and he turned those over to the police.

Tonight is the busiest night at the club and I can't wait to get through it because we're booking our vacation this weekend. We have been talking about different locations we could quickly fly to for a few days' getaway. I've chosen where I want to go but haven't told him yet. I figured he's always surprising me with things so I wanted to surprise him this time. I have bought some things to model for him later tonight hoping he can guess where I want to go. I hope he's as excited as I am.

"Hey, love, dinner is ready!" he calls.

It's so great having a man that doesn't mind cooking, and he does a great job of it too. I'm not talking boxed mac and cheese shit; I'm talking roasts and pastas, good home-cooked meals.

"I'm coming, sweetie!" I run down the stairs already dressed for work and straight up to my man and give him a kiss. "This smells so good, and you look so yummy."

"You keep talking like that and we're not going to make it to work on time and I'm going to rip another pair of panties."

I pout. "But I'm hungry."

He laughs. "I've already made your plate."

Taking a seat at the snack bar, he places my plate in front of me, but I notice he's distracted. "What's wrong, sweetie?" I ask,

"I've been thinking about doing something and I'm hoping you'll be on board with it."

I raise my eyebrows at his genuine nervousness. "What is it?"

He turns to face me with his plate in hand and has a seat on the side of me. "I want to open a new

210

club and train you to run Thrive."

"Are you sure I'm the best person to run it? Why not Shane or Jonah?"

"I love you, Skyler, and I would like to make you my wife. Why would I want one of them to run it and not my wife? I have no doubt you can handle it. Everyone at the club loves you, and they all know you can hold your own, so you won't have an issue earning respect. And to be perfectly honest, making you manager instead of one of the other guys frees you to help me from time to time with the new one."

I nod thinking it over. "It would be a cool project for the two of us to work on. Why did you think I would be leery?"

"I'm thinking about making it a...strip club." I laugh because I don't know how else to respond. "Why are you laughing?"

"Sorry, sweetie, it's because I didn't see that coming and it threw me off."

"So you're not opposed to it?"

I shrug. "We *are* in LA. It isn't like it would be the first strip club around."

"That's the thing; a lot of the strip clubs around here are cheesy and slimy. I want a sexy, classy, nice strip club where we could bring in everyday clients but also have expensive VIP sections for anyone who wants to be discreet."

"I actually like the idea. I want to be in charge of the dancers though."

"That's fine. I want to have a choreographer work with them. I don't like the idea of them coming up with their own routine."

"This is so good! I agree. It has to flow, and you need a good DJ too, someone who's good with music and a mic."

"For sure. Okay, when we get back from vacation, we start looking for locations. Do you want to keep singing or do you want to get more involved in the clubs with me?"

"I'm not sure. I mean, I came out here to sing, but I love being in the club life with you. I'm fine if I only do a random gig here and there. Maybe I can fill in if Mikey needs someone once in a while."

"Whatever you want, love. I want you to be happy, and if that means working the clubs with me, fine. If it means singing, I'm fine with that too."

"I enjoy singing, but I don't have the outgoing personality for it. I'm way more comfortable behind the bar and in the club. I've come to realize I was really chasing happiness, and I think I've found it."

"Good, because we've got to get cleaned up and head to work."

I laugh at his abrupt halt to our conversation. "I love you, Logan Michaels." I kiss him and put my dish in the sink then run upstairs to get my shoes.

***

Logan

We're the first ones in the club, which is good because I want to go over inventory with Skyler. I get my clipboard and head to the back room to look over what we have on hand and create a list of what we will need. I talk with her about what we go through most of and how much I usually order. I also talk about how long it takes for stuff to come in, so I don't wait until we are too low on certain items.

"Wine is selling but mainly on singles night when everyone is here to hook up and wants to look classy. We sell a lot of Pinot, Chardonnay, Moscato, Shiraz, and Pinot Noir, so I'll lighten up on ordering the others and order more of those."

"What are you going to do with the others if we don't sell them?"

"They are higher end wines so I'm hoping to move them to the new club and sell them there. If not I'll remove them from inventory and you and I can try them."

"That is a lot of wine. I guess we could serve it at our Monday night dinners. Kind of like a wine tasting, or maybe we host a wine tasting event on Sunday evening?"

"That's not a bad idea, my love." I lean in to kiss Skyler on her luscious lips. "Let me show you how to place the order before we get carried away in here."

We head back to my office to sit down at the computer. I show her how I place the order for all the liquor and how to check on what's arriving.

"If you order it today, it will usually be here by next Wednesday or Thursday, so you should have it before the next busy weekend."

"Got it."

"I usually check the inventory on Friday or Saturday, depending on how busy I am around the club, but you should place the order by Saturday."

I finish placing the order. "If there is ever a question about over ordering, I would rather you order too much than us run out of something. Staff should be arriving to make sure the bars are stocked and the fruit trays are full. You already know this part so it'll be easy, and Shane is kick ass at making sure the bars run smoothly, so check in on them but let him do his job."

"I like Shane, and I'm glad that if I'm going to help you run this place I have him on my team."

I glance at the camera and see Shane walking in; I pick up my phone and shoot him a text.

Logan: Can you come to my office?

Shane: On my way.

A moment later there is a knock on my door.

"Come in."

"Hey, boss, what's up? Hey, Sky!"

"Hi, Shane," Skyler replies.

"Hey, Shane. Have a seat." He looks nervous. "Relax," I say, "you're not in trouble or anything. As the assistant manager I need to inform you of some small changes."

"Okay."

"Skyler and I have been talking, and once we get back from our vacation we plan on opening another club. I would like you to help her manage this one while I get the other one running. She'll be bouncing back and forth because she's going to manage the dancers at the other club. She'll be doing all the ordering for this club, and the two of you can work out any issues or come to me with any problems you're not sure how to solve."

"Cool!"

"Now, of course that means a pay raise, because I'm not going to leave you two to run the club without giving you more money. I would like to make you a salaried employee and pay you $40,000.00 per year to start. Depending on what happens with the second club, you may eventually get promoted to manager and I'll pay you more. Is that cool?"

"Hell yeah!" Shane jumps up and shakes Skyler's hand. "We'll make a great team," he says enthusiastically.

"Good," Skyler says with a grin, "because I told Logan if there was anyone I wanted helping me, it was you."

"Thanks, Sky. Thanks, Logan." He fist bumps me and walks out of my office to get to work.

There's one more knock on the door and it is Tony and Jake wondering what their positions are tonight. I inform them that Sky is on bar two, and one of them should be close by while the other is wandering.

Sky says, "I'm going to go start setting up my bar for tonight. I'll see you in a little bit." She gives me a kiss and walks out of my office with her security team.

The music is playing and patrons are filing in, hoping to have a good time tonight. Within an hour my club is packed and there's a line down the street of people waiting to get in. I have some VIP sections booked tonight with Shawna managing them well. I make my rounds to visit my VIPs and introduce myself, making sure they are happy with the service they're receiving from Shawna and my other staff. Once I'm sure everyone is pleased, I head down to the bar to check on my bar staff. They're good, and I knew they would be because Shane is running tonight.

Then I hear Jonah in my ear wig. "Logan, Troy just tried to enter the club."

I respond right away. "Did you stop him?"

"Yeah, but he's pissed. Said he's going to sue you for not allowing him in."

I laugh. "Fuck him. It's private property. I can refuse entrance to whomever I want."

He laughs back. "Just a heads up."

"Thanks, I appreciate that, man. Let me know if anything else suspicious comes up."

"I'm heading around the club now to scope things out and make sure everything looks good. I'll let you know if I see anything."

I head back to my office to shoot off an email to my agent, letting her know we want another property and that I would like a list of places available in the next two weeks. I'm also sure to inform her that we have decided to go strip club instead of dance club.

I'm hoping Sky and I can come up with a name while we're relaxing on vacation somewhere. It's kind of driving me crazy that she won't tell me where she wants to go until tonight. I've been asking her for about two weeks and she keeps saying she has to think about it. When she finally chose a location, she said she had a fun way to surprise me. I can't wait to get her home tonight and see what she has in mind so we can book the vacation tomorrow.

I get a call that one of the bars needs help, so I head back out to see what's going on. Shane is behind the second bar with Kelly and Skyler, and bar one is way overloaded. They tell me they need liquor and a hand behind the bar. This place is jumping tonight. I run to the back to grab what they need and hurry back to jump in and help out. I don't usually like being behind the bar, but tonight it's a welcome distraction.

When we're finally wrapping up last call, I leave the first bar and head over to the second to check on them. Shane tells me they're good, that he's running to stock them on liquor while they start cleaning up. I make one more round through my VIP section to see who's left up there, and most of them have cleared out. There's a large drunk crowd up here that Shawna probably should have cut off a long time ago.

"Jonah," I call over the mic, "VIP 3 is filled with a drunken bachelor party and I need them to be cleared out. Get them all cabs or whatever, but I want them gone."

"I'm on it."

In minutes I see him appearing with one of my other bouncers to get these guys out of here.

People slowly make their way out of the club and the crowd is dwindling. The DJ has already started gradually lowering the music volume, letting people know the night is coming to an end. That usually helps to empty the place as well.

Jonah comes over a short while later to let me know they are making final rounds but he thinks the club is empty.

"I'm going to check the ladies room!" Skyler calls and walks off in that direction. When Tony gets up to follow her, she says, "I'm good. There's no one here."

He nods and takes his place back at the bar. My staff is cleaning up and I don't see any patrons, so unless anyone is in the bathroom or passed out in a corner—which has happened—we're good to lock the doors.

I press the button on my ear wig to give Jonah the okay to lock up, and as he's about to lock the door we hear a loud bang, and a fire breaks out behind the bar where Kelly and Skyler were working.

I scream for everyone to get out of the club before the fire spreads. With all the open alcohol behind there, this place can go up quick. The staff quickly makes their way to the door. I'm watching to see where the fire goes when I realize Skyler hasn't come out yet.

"Jonah!" I shout. "Skyler is in the bathroom!"

I can already hear the fire trucks because Shane called as I was clearing the place. Jonah and I run toward the ladies room, but bottles of liquor are exploding and glass is flying all over the place. The smoke is getting thick, and the only way to get to her is through the back door. Jonah tries to pull me from the club, but I'm fighting him.

"Logan, the fire department is pulling up! We'll show them how to get to her!"

I'm totally freaking out because my love is stuck in a burning building and I'm afraid I'll never see her again. Jonah runs up to the fire chief and frantically explains that we have someone still inside. He tells him that she's in the ladies room and takes them to the back door, informing them this is the safest way to get to her.

My two security guys stop me from running after them. "They'll get her!" Tony shouts as the firemen run in the back entrance. All I keep thinking in my head is, *Please be okay, please be okay.*

"What the fuck is taking them so long!" I scream to no one in particular.

Shane is by my side with Jonah. "Give them a minute. I know it feels like an eternity, but they've only been in there a few minutes." Shane squeezes my shoulder, trying to comfort me, but it isn't working. An ambulance pulls up, and I'm hoping it's because they called for it and they have found her.

The doors burst open and a firefighter comes out with Sky over his shoulder. She's unconscious. He lays her down on the stretcher that meets him halfway, and they start working on her.

"Go with her," Shane says. "We'll meet you at the hospital as soon as this place is under control."

I run after the EMT, jump in the back, and explain that I'm her boyfriend, that she has no other family, and they let me ride with them. It's only then I'm informed that I have some cuts on my hands and face I'll need to have cleaned and dressed when we get to the hospital. I explain about the shards of flying glass from the alcohol bottles.

I'm pacing the waiting room waiting for some update on Skyler when my entire team comes rushing through the doors of the hospital. They can sense the stress and panic as soon as they see me.

"I don't know anything yet," I mournfully inform them.

We all sit in painful silence, praying she makes it. I look around at this group, and it's in this moment that I realize how awesome our friends are.

Chapter 16

Skyler

There are multiple voices around me, but I can only make out a few because there's too much noise. I hear Logan talking to someone and I think it's Jonah. Though I want to open my eyes to see where I am and who's around me, I just can't manage it. I'm scared. Why can't I open my eyes? Why do I hurt?

I drift back into a darkness I don't even understand why I'm in.

I try to groan, so I can get someone's attention. I feel someone on the side of me. It hurts to open my eyes, so I'm not even sure who is here until I hear his voice. It's Logan, and he sounds like he's been crying. I want to tell him it's okay, but I can't manage the words.

"You're going to be okay, my love," he whispers. "Rest. I'm here for you and I love you." I feel him kiss my hand before I drift off again.

I wake to more voices.

"Doc, she started to grumble before but didn't really say anything. When do you think she'll wake up?"

"It's hard to say. From the x-rays we took, it appears she was hit over the head pretty hard before she was placed in the bathroom. Give her a little more time. She'll wake when she's ready. She's lucky you have a good sprinkler system and the fire department got there when they did."

I will myself to wake up. I have questions because I don't remember any fire or being hit on the head. I can't open my eyes. I squeeze my hand the best I can to let Logan know I hear him and I'm not giving up.

Sadie is crying, asking Logan how someone could do this to me. She takes my hand. "Skyler, please wake up! So many people love you and want to hear your beautiful voice again."

"I'm sure my voice is not sounding so beautiful right now," I manage in a low, gravelly tone.

"Oh thank God, you're awake!" Sadie cries, squeezing my hand.

"You're making my hand soggy."

"I'm sorry." She giggles with excitement. "Be right back." I hear her run to the hall and call, "Logan, she's awake."

He comes running in with Sadie. "Sky?" he questions, and I can hear panic in his voice.

"I'm here, sweetie," I whisper.

"Oh thank God."

"Welcome back to us, Miss Jones," the doctor says. "Do you know where you are?"

"Hospital."

"Good. Do you know why you're in the hospital?"

I shake my head and instantly regret it. "Oh, that hurts."

"I'm sure it does. Miss Jones, do you remember anything from the other night?"

"Other night?" I ask in panic. "How long have I been here?"

"Miss Jones, I need you to calm down. If you don't remember, that's okay, but if you get worked up I may have to sedate you, and I would rather not do that."

I take a few deep breaths. "Fine. How long have I been here?"

"You've been here a few days now, and once you stay awake and we're sure you have recovered from your concussion, I can send you home."

"Okay. Can someone tell me what happened?"

"As long as you promise to remain calm. If your monitors start to beep, I'm kicking everyone out." I nod and he tells me he'll be back in a bit.

***

Logan

"I'm so glad you're back, Sky. How does your head feel?"

"My head and chest hurt a bit, but that's it. Will you tell me what happened?"

"We were closing the bar the other night," I say quietly. "Somehow Billy got through security. Troy had tried but Jonah caught him and told him to hit the road."

"Who let Billy in?"

"Don't worry about him. He's been fired. Anyway, he planted a small bomb behind the bar you were working. We assume he was figuring once it went off, the entire club would go up."

I pause, watching her take a few deep breaths. "Are you okay?"

"Yes, keep going."

"Before he set it off, he hit you on the back of the head and dragged you off to the ladies room, probably figuring we wouldn't notice you missing until it was too late. He wasn't accounting for you telling me you were heading that way."

Sky takes a few more deep breaths. She's having a hard time listening to this, so I wait until I see she's composed before I continue.

"The police found his truck up the street from the club with all the equipment he used to make the bomb in the back of it. He's been arrested and will be fully charged with arson and attempted murder. You'll never have to worry about him again. They think Troy is also involved but don't have the proof they need just yet to arrest him, though they're pretty sure Billy will flip once they start talking to him."

"Hawaii," Sky says.

I look at her in confusion. "What do you mean Hawaii?"

She chuckles. "That's where I want to go. I want to go to Hawaii. Please tell me you'll take me there?"

"My love, I'll take you to the moon if that's

where you want to go. Hawaii it is. As soon as you're well enough to travel we'll head there." I smile down at her and brush her hair away from her face.

"Logan, I want to go home and rest in my own bed." she says, opening her eyes.

"There are those pretty eyes," I say with a huge smile as Sadie walks back in with Jonah.

"Sky, I'm so sorry this happened." Jonah sighs in frustration. "The guy who let Billy in has been fired. He wasn't paying attention and allowed him to walk in with a hooded sweatshirt on so he was able to hide the bomb in his front pocket."

"Jonah, this isn't your fault, and I won't have you beating yourself up over it. Which bouncer was it?" Skyler asks curiously.

"It was Nick, why?"

"Isn't he the same person who let Troy in the night that Logan had to kick him back out? I'm wondering if he let Billy in on purpose."

"You're right, Skyler. It was Nick that let him in. He said he didn't know what to do because Troy was putting up a stink, but I bet he did it on purpose," I tell her, confirming her suspicion. "I bet Troy and Billy paid Nick to let them in the club, and Troy would have made it in if Jonah wasn't at the door to stop him."

Kyle, Shauna, and Kelly all walk into the room.

"I'm so glad to see you awake. How are you feeling?" Kelly asks with a big smile.

"Thanks for coming, guys. The doctor said I may be able to get out of here in a few days, which will be nice. I want to get into my own bed and onto the vacation I was supposed to be planning this week." She winces. "Sorry, my head still hurts. I have to remember to talk slow and low."

Kelly rubs her leg. "We'll whisper, though I have a feeling the doctor is going to kick us out because he was giving us looks as we walked in."

"I'll tell him I need a few more minutes with you guys and then I'll get my rest."

"You need to eat too, Sky. It's already after lunchtime. When he comes back we'll see what you can have for dinner and then you can go back to sleep." I'm hoping she's hungry and will be willing to put some food in her stomach.

A few minutes later, the doctor comes walking in and wants to kick everybody out. Skyler begs for a little bit more time with her friends, and the doctor agrees to ten more minutes. I take the opportunity to ask the doctor about what she can have for dinner. She hasn't eaten in days. He tells me he'll be back with a dinner menu in ten minutes when it's time for everybody to leave.

Exactly ten minutes later, the doctor walks back in. "Okay it's time for everybody to go. Skyler needs her rest so she can be sent home tomorrow or the day after."

Everyone hugs her and says goodbye as they head out the door. Skyler looks tired from the visit, but she also seems happy to have had a few minutes with her friends. Only Sadie and Jonah are left, and he's trying to convince me to go home and shower, telling me they'll stay with Skyler while I go, but I don't want to leave her side.

"Maybe after she eats I'll go."

"Logan, go home and shower." Sky yawns. "I don't want a stinky boyfriend."

I burst out laughing. "Oh, so now I'm stinky, am I?"

"I tried to tell you, man, but you don't want to listen to me. Listen to your girlfriend. Go take a shower."

"Okay, okay, I'll go home and shower. I'll be back as soon as I can. Is there anything you want from home?"

"Yeah, I would like a toothbrush and a fresh-smelling boyfriend."

"You're funny now, huh? I'll be back as soon." I kiss her on the forehead. "I love you, Skyler."

"I love you too, Logan."

She closes her eyes, exhausted from her short visit with her friends.

"Jonah, keep an eye on my girl and don't let anything happen to her."

"You got it. Sadie and I'll be right here, and if her dinner comes before you get back, we'll try to get her to eat for you too."

"Cool, thanks." We bump fists and I run out the door. Yeah, I literally run because I want to get back to the hospital as quick as I can. I'm so whipped.

Chapter 17

Skyler

I'm lying in bed alone and the aroma in the house tells me Logan is cooking. That man is amazing; I have been out of the hospital for three weeks now and he's done nothing but work and take care of me. The club is closed right now for repairs. It's important we get the club open again as quickly as possible, so he's been busting his tail working with the insurance company and the construction company to get everything done.

The good news is Billy rolled on Troy. They were in it together and the police didn't need them to confess to paying Nick because they were dumb enough to leave a paper trail, so he's being arrested as well. The three of them will be in jail for a while, and that's fine by me. Now Logan and I can leave on our vacation without fear of what we will come home to.

We leave tonight on a redeye to Hawaii and will arrive first thing in the morning. Logan has booked us an all-inclusive resort right on the beach. He says he's also booked some surprises for me. That has become the new game with us, who can surprise who with what. It's a bit silly but it's fun, and I wouldn't have it any other way.

I hear Logan walking up the stairs. I pretend I'm still sleeping so I can see what he'll do to wake me up. He pulls the blankets down to find my shirt has ridden up and my belly is hanging out. I lay there until I feel something cold on my belly. I yelp and he cracks up laughing.

"I knew you weren't sleeping. You had a smile on your face the entire time."

"Maybe I was having a nice dream and you ruined it," I pout.

"Oh baby, let me make your dreams come true." He leans down and licks the whip cream off my belly. I moan to let him know I'm enjoying this and hope he'll continue this little game. He lifts me off the bed and pulls my shorts and thong down. I'm glad he has eased up on ripping them.

He tosses them to the side and takes an ice cube from the bowl I hadn't seen him bring up. He runs it from my belly button straight down to my pubic hair and onto my clit. I whimper because it's almost painful. He rubs it over my hardened nub for a few more moments before he dips his tongue down and laps up the water, and the mix of the cold from the ice and heat from his tongue is driving me mad. He laughs as I squirm against his mouth.

"I could eat this for breakfast, lunch and dinner."

"Please let me come, Logan. It's been too long."

He stops to look at me. "Love, we are leaving on

vacation. You're not going to stop coming." For the first time in a long time, I blush. He gives me his devilish grin before he dives back in devouring my pussy like it's his favorite feast. I'm moaning and grinding my hips when he pins me down with his hands and continues to lick my clit. I'm getting close to an orgasm, so as usual he stops and sticks his tongue as deep inside me as he can so I explode on his tongue. I try to move, but he won't let me until he's done lapping up every last drop.

He takes another ice cube and rubs it over my nipples and they get even harder than they were. I didn't even think it was possible, but they're so hard they hurt.

"Logan," I moan. "Please, that's too cold, suck them."

"Gladly." He palms my breast and fits as much of it as he can into his mouth. While he's sucking on it I hear a vibration, though I don't realize what it is until presses it gently against my clit. "Logan!"

"I got you, love, just relax."

"It's so sensitive."

He bites my nipple. "I know, let it go love," he says, but I can't; I'm on sensation overload. "Love, please give me what I want and I'll give you what you want." He kisses me passionately. His tongue is attacking mine when my orgasm tears through me and my legs tighten around his hand. His kiss is blocking my screams as I ride out my orgasm. He finally pulls away and I close my eyes, trying to slow my breath.

He climbs on top of me and slowly slides his entire length in me. He slowly slips himself out of me and then back in, teasing me.

"Logan, give it to me!" I demand. He slides it in a bit faster this time, still not giving me what I want. "Logan, you promised," I whine. He pulls out and rams into me hard then pauses deep inside me.

"Is that what you want?" I bite my lip and nod. He pulls out slowly and ram into me again. He's hitting so deep I whimper. He's gradually picking up the pace, slamming me just as deep and it feels unbelievable. "Yes, Logan, like that."

"Skyler, love, I'm not going to last much longer, so give me what I want. Milk me, baby!" He keeps going harder and faster and I give him what he wants. Another orgasm is ripping through me and I'm milking him, begging for his seed. He slams in me one last time and freezes there as he empties every last drop deep inside me.

***

Logan

I nudge Skyler awake. She stretches and flashes her beautiful brown eyes at me. "Where are we?"

"I must have tired you out because you slept the entire flight. We'll be landing in about twenty minutes."

She sits up and stretches, taking her water bottle from the seat pouch in front of her and taking a long drink. We are landing at 7:00am, and I have paid extra money for early check in because I want our room available when we get there. I have a few surprises planned for her when we get off the plane.

I want this to be the trip of her dreams.

When the seatbelt light goes off we stand, and being in first class we're let off the plane first. We head off with our carry-ons in hand toward baggage claim. There's a man in a suit waiting for us with a sign that reads **'Michaels'** on it.

Her eyes light up full of excitement. "Is that for us?" Skyler asks, and I nod. We walk over to him and the gentleman presents her with a beautiful floral lei.

"Aloha, ma'am," he says, placing the lei around her neck. Her smile is so big I'm sure her cheeks hurt.

He gives me a lei as well and greets me. My lei is blue and yellow flowers and hers are pretty pink flowers.

"Mr. Michaels, your luggage is being pulled off the plane right now. If you'll wait here I'll retrieve it and we can be on our way."

I thank him and he walks off to get our luggage.

"Can I take a selfie of us to send to Sadie? She pretty much hates me right now, and I want to brag."

I kiss her. "Anything you want. This trip is all about you."

We lean together, and she stretches her hand out in front of us and takes a picture, then quickly sends it off to Sadie. By the time she's done texting, our driver is back with our bags. He takes Skyler's carry on and hangs it over his shoulder, instructing us to follow him. As we're driving through Hawaii we're pointing out sights and looking at different fun things we want to check out.

It takes us about forty-five minutes to get to the hotel. The driver parks, opens the door for Skyler, and then walks us in with our luggage. I walk up to the counter, give my name, and instantly the clerk's expression changes.

"Oh yes, Mr. Michaels. We have your room all set for you. Please follow me and I'll show you the way." She tells concierge to take our bags to our room immediately. I hand our driver a one hundred dollar bill and thank him for getting us here. We follow our guide to our room, and she's pointing out the spa, the gym, and the different pools around the complex. She informs us of the shops out front and the different restaurants around it. We also have a special beachside cabana booked that she informs me is ready for our use whenever we want it.

When we arrive at our room, she inserts the key into the lock on the double doors and opens them to a huge suite that has an incredible open layout. There's a large living area and kitchen with dining table. The balcony is huge with cushioned wicker furniture and a glass top table. We walk over, open the doors, and step out.

"Logan, this view is breathtaking." Skyler takes some pictures with her phone. We have a clear view of the beach, beautiful palm trees, and the bluest ocean you'll ever see.

"Is there anything else I can get you before I leave you to enjoy your stay with us?"

"No, ma'am," I say to the hotel clerk. "Thank you. I think we are good from here."

"If there's anything you need or we can do to make your stay better, please feel free to press zero on your phone and we'll take care of it right away."

"Thank you."

She heads toward the doors, closing them behind her.

"So, my love, what do you want to do today?"

"I have no idea. There's too much to choose from I don't know where to begin," Skyler replies with her big, heart stopping smile.

"Well let me tell you some of the things I already have planned for us. We'll be going on a full day island tour this week. I have his and her massages planned for us, and you can't come to Hawaii without going to a luau, so we'll be doing that as well."

"I think I want to relax on the beach for now."

"We can do that, but we need to come back to shower and get ready for our dinner cruise. It's going out on the water at 5:00."

There's a knock on the door; our luggage has arrived. I slip the bellhop a tip while Skyler wheels our bags into the room.

"Perfect timing," she says. She opens her suitcase to get her bikini and beach cover up, running into the bathroom to change while I dig mine out. She comes out in this Hawaiian print pink and white bikini, and she looks absolutely stunning. She collects a tube of sunscreen, a towel, and a bottle of water to take down to the beach.

When we get to the edge of the beach, we find a man standing in a booth for the cabanas. I give him my name, ask him which cabana is ours. He walks us over to it, informing us that there's soda, water, and seltzer in the fridge, and points out there are towels on the shelf. We look inside, shocked at how big and spacious it is. There are two lounge chairs waiting for us. Skyler takes her chair and slides it outside so she's in the sun, and I do the same with mine. I take her tube of sunscreen, squirt some into my hands, and run it all over her back and shoulders.

"If you burn, I won't be able to touch you later and that will be a big problem."

She kisses me and says, "Thank you," before lying on her chair in the hot Hawaiian sun.

***

Skyler

Logan has been the absolute best all day today. He has been so attentive, making sure I've had plenty of sunscreen on. I've been drinking plenty of fluids so I don't dehydrate, and he ordered lunch to be delivered to us on the beach. We took a few quick dips in the ocean to cool off; the sun here is brutal. It has been the most relaxing afternoon of lounging around and reading on the beach.

When it's time for us to leave to get ready for dinner, we put our chairs back into our cabana, drop our dirty towels into a bin, put our sandals on, and head back to our room. The sand is unbelievably soft but way too hot to walk on without sandals. You can maybe take a few steps here and there, but you would literally burn your feet without them.

We take the long way back to the room so we can take a look around at the little shops. The entire outside of the village is populated with restaurants, jewelry shops, clothing stores, and local crafters selling their own trinkets.

"Is there something you like, love?"

I shake my head. "I'm ready to head back to the room. It's hot and I want to take a cool shower and get ready for dinner."

We're all showered and dressed for dinner. Logan looks nice in his khaki shorts and polo shirt, and I'm wearing a pretty floral sundress that matches his shirt. I'm pretty sure when he told our personal shopper we needed clothes for Hawaii she matched us on purpose. We walk down to the concierge to find out where we need to go to get on our dinner cruise. He calls a car and tells the man where we're going, we climb in, and he whisks us away to our location.

When we arrive Logan steps out of the car, tips the driver, and we walk up the dock to board the ferry. There's a man at the entrance to whom we give our names and show our tickets. He lets us on the boat and tells us to enjoy our night. There are a bunch of round tables everywhere, and diners are expected to share a table with other couples or families. We locate our seats and we're the first from our table to arrive. Our waiter arrives to take our drink order and leaves. While he's getting them, we discuss walking back up to the main deck to look around and enjoy the gorgeous weather. Within minutes our waiter is back with our beverages.

We thank him and take our drinks to the main deck to watch people aboard the boat. There's also a bar up here where we can refill our drinks and some small tables to sit and relax.

A short time later the boat pulls away from the dock and the captain comes over the intercom and asking us to take our seats for dinner. He informs us that the cruise is about two hours and after dinner we'll go to the main deck for a beautiful firework display.

A waiter comes over and tells us to please help ourselves to the buffet, so we head up to the line and find a huge variety of local cuisine. I don't know where to start. We both try different foods so we can sample things from each other's plates and head back to our table. We have two other couples sitting with us. One couple is from the East Coast and is there on their honeymoon. The other couple is a fun older couple that has been married for a few years and decided they needed a vacation and had always wanted to come to Hawaii. The older couple is at the end of their trip, but the younger couple just got here like us and is looking forward to the rest of their trip. We all share about where we want to go and visit and the older couple shares where they've gone and what they liked about each of their experiences.

Once we have finished eating, the six of us continue our night up on the main deck. I order another glass of wine and we find a table at the front of the boat where we'll be able to have a direct view of the fireworks. I brought a sweater to put on over my dress and I'm glad because it's a bit chilly out on the water.

The upper deck is filling as more people finish

their dinners and come outside. It must be just about time for the fireworks because we only have a short time left on the boat. Suddenly there's a large boom in the sky and it lights up. Logan reaches over for my hand and I lean my head on his shoulder to watch the display lighting up the sky. It's absolutely spectacular and a perfect way to end the night.

"I love you, Skyler," he whispers in my ear.

I turn to him and smile. "I love you too, Logan."

Chapter 18

Skyler

This has been the most incredible five days of my life. We have done so many wonderful things together and Logan has done nothing but fulfill my every wish. We've done everything from snorkeling, to swimming with dolphins, to enjoying a day at the spa. One of my favorite parts of the trip was the tour we went on. We visited Pearl Harbor, the *USS Missouri*, a pineapple plantation, a nut farm, and we were taken to see stunning beaches, lookout points, volcanic craters, and lush rainforests. Our tour guide filled us in on all the history from around the island, telling us about movies filmed there, the history of some of the buildings, rich sides of the island versus poor sides of the island. Hawaii is a truly beautiful place to live.

Today we have decided to take it easy before we have to fly back home. Logan says he has one more special night planned for me and we can do whatever I want for the day. I want to walk up the beach to have lunch at a beachside restaurant. The food is fresh and delicious. We've eaten there a few times throughout the week. We walk down the beach hand in hand.

"Did you enjoy your time here?" Logan asks me.

"Of course, it was the best. Thank you for such a wonderful time."

"You're so welcome, my love. Hopefully this will be the first of many trips we can take together. I want to show you the world, baby."

We arrive at the restaurant and request an outdoor table so we can sit on the beach for one last meal. I'm hoping it waits to rain until we are done eating. If there's one thing I've learned this week is that it'll rain at some point every day. It's usually early in the day, but since it hasn't rained yet I'm betting it will come soon. It's not like the rain at home, though, because it stays sunny while it rains and it's a warm rain with a rainbow immediately following. We walk around the area after lunch to check out some shops. We come across a Coach store, Michael Kors, a Ferrari dealership, and many other shops. Logan pulls me into the Michael Kors store and insists I need a new bag. We walk through and I pick a nice black leather satchel that set him back almost four hundred dollars. I'm quite shocked but I have learned not to argue with him. The clerk wraps my bag up and places it in a paper shopping bag and we head on our way.

When we finally get back to the room, there's a bag hanging in our room from a hook.

"What is that?" I ask him, confused because it

wasn't there when we left.

"A dress I had delivered for you to wear tonight."

"Where are we going?"

He smiles. "I rented out the beach around our cabana for a special candlelit dinner for two."

I can't help the smile that spreads across my cheeks. "You did not."

"I absolutely did, so go get showered and changed because we need to be downstairs at 5:45."

I kiss him and run off to shower.

***

Logan

It's our last night here and I plan on making it perfect. I have rented a large section of the beach that is being roped off so no one can enter but us, and I'm having a special dinner delivered. I also have arranged for some lights to be hung around our cabana and tiki torches stuck into the sand for some nice lighting. Now I need to get my clothes and the rest of what I need to make the night complete.

I get my button down short sleeve shirt and my shorts from the closet and tuck her last surprise into my pocket to keep it hidden from spying eyes. I jump in the other shower, ensuring I'm ready when Skyler gets out. I shower quickly, run some gel through my hair, and shave with my electric razor that I brought for touch ups.

When I walk out of the second bathroom Skyler is standing there wearing a white strapless dress that looks absolutely amazing on her. It's an elegant white lace dress the front comes just above her knees while the back goes down to her calves. She's wearing fancy sandals that I know she'll take off because she loves walking in the sand in the evening once it has cooled down a bit. I take her hand. "Are you ready?" She nods. "You look beautiful. This dress is stunning on you and you have a gorgeous tan." She blushes. "Come on, I don't want to be late."

Actually I'm nervous about this last surprise and I'm hoping it doesn't show. Tonight is the night I plan on showing her how much she truly means to me.

We leave our room and head down to the beach. As we walk by the concierge hand in hand he winks at me, letting me know everything is set up and it's safe to keep going. I continue past him like I have seen nothing. We get down to the beach and Skyler freezes in her tracks, taking it all in. The hotel has done an amazing job. The ropes have been made out of Hawaiian flowers like they do the leis, and there is a large amount of space around our cabana so we can have our privacy, which is good because I plan on making love to her in that cabana after dinner. The tiki torches are perfectly scattered throughout, making it very romantic, and there's a table by the water with a two chairs and a candle in the middle.

"Logan, this is breathtaking." A tear slips down her cheek.

"Come on, love." I pull her toward the table where there are some musicians playing Hawaiian music. We sit at our table, and the water is so close we can almost touch it but the tide is going out so we don't have to worry about getting soaked. I keep patting my pocket to confirm I didn't lose what I'm carrying and I hope she doesn't notice.

Three waiters come over, two bringing our meals, and one carrying a bottle of wine. They fill our glasses and place our meals on the table then disappear to give us privacy. While the food looks delicious, I'm so nervous I can hardly eat. I force down as much as I can so as not to give anything away.

"This is delicious," Skyler says. "Everything has been perfect this week. Thank you again, Logan. I couldn't have asked for a better vacation."

"It was my pleasure. I wanted you to be able to relax and enjoy yourself. This vacation has allowed us to do that and for me to spoil you a little too."

She raises her eyebrows. "Spoil me a little? How about spoil me a *lot*. You have treated me to so many surprises, made love to me daily as promised, and now you're finishing it off with this beautiful dinner on the beach. Logan, I couldn't think of anything that would have made this trip better."

He gives me a sideways grin. "I can think of one more thing that would make this trip absolutely perfect."

"Oh yeah? What is that?"

I pull out the ring and get down on one knee. Skyler knows what I'm doing because her hands have already covered her mouth in shock.

"Skyler Jones, I love you so much and want to spend the rest of my life making you happy and spoiling you the way I have this week. I want you to

243

live your life never having to worry about a single thing again. Will you please end this trip perfectly by making me the happiest man on this Earth and be my wife?"

She's sobbing, but she nods. I slip the ring on her shaking left finger, and when I stand so does she, embracing me. We kiss and I'm thinking *thank god she said yes*. I ask her to turn around because there's a photographer standing there that has been taking pictures of our entire dinner and proposal. The picture he's taking right now is us on the beach with the sun practically set behind us and I'm sure it will be a gorgeous memory.

We sit back down when the waiters are removing our dinner plates and bringing our desserts.

"Logan, I can't believe you planned all of this. It's so magical. Thank you."

"Skyler, I mean it. I want to marry you, and sooner rather than later. I don't mind if we wait until after Sadie and Jonah so we don't steal their thunder, but I want to be married soon."

"I don't care if we get married in the club with our friends. It's not like I have family here. You and our club friends are my family, so it won't take a ton of planning as far as I'm concerned."

"Good. We'll start planning as soon as we get back. Since we're not planning a big elaborate wedding, it won't matter if we marry before Jonah and Sadie, because their wedding will be quite different from ours."

When we finished dessert, I take her by the hand to dance with her on the beach.

"You have changed my life forever and I'm so

thankful." I brush her hair from her face, place my hand at her nape, and pull her in for a kiss. She opens to me and deepens the kiss, and that's when I notice the music is fading because the musicians are walking down the beach playing to give us our privacy. I pull her into our cabana and the lawn chair is laid flat with rose petals sprinkled all over it. I slip her dress down her body. She's standing before me in a white thong and matching bra. I grin and for the sake of ritual I rip the panties off of her and she cracks up laughing.

I remove her bra. "Lie down, my love."

She walks the few steps to the lawn chair and lies down. Luckily for me these lawn chairs are huge and we both fit on one. I kiss her slowly and passionately because I want her to truly feel the love I have for her tonight. I kiss my way up her jaw to her ear. I use the tip of my tongue to lick down the vein in her neck to her collarbone. I take her breast in my hand and massage it for a minute. My hand glides slowly up and down her body. "You have the softest skin. It's flawless." I take her nipple in my mouth, sucking it. I gently run the tips of my fingers down her stomach and to her folds. Her hips grind against my hand as I gently start rubbing her clit. I can feel it has hardened when I pinch it lightly between my thumb and forefinger.

She moans quietly. "Fuck, Logan."

I laugh. "We will, love, I promise." I dip my head to take her nipple again. This time I bite it and her hips jolt up to grind against my hand. I slide two fingers deep inside her and that's all it takes to send her over the edge. Her muscles tighten around my fingers while I curl them deep inside her. I can't wait for my cock to feel the same thing. I quickly pull my fingers out of her and stand to remove my shorts.

I straddle the chair with her legs wrapped around my waist, lean forward, and place one hand on each side of her. I slip my cock inside of her, picking my hips up slightly, I start sliding my entire length in and out of her.

"Yes, Logan. This feels so good."

I continue hammering into her, fighting to maintain control until she releases, but I truly won't last much longer. "Come on, Sky, let me have it." And just like that she does. I hammer her a few more times as her tight little pussy milks me for all I've got. "Yes, Sky!" I scream and then collapse on top of her.

We lay on the lawn chair in silence for a few moments, enjoying our time together. Once we've caught our breath, I lean up on one arm.

"Do you like the ring I picked for you?"

She picks up her left hand and looks at it. "It's beautiful."

I bought her a one carat diamond with pink diamonds wrapped around it so it would match the promise ring she wears on her right hand.

"I have to admit, I wasn't expecting all of this when you said you had one last surprise for me. I can't wait to get home and tell our friends."

"You can show them all at our Monday night dinner."

"We're still having it? I thought we were going to skip this week?"

"Nah, I just said that. I was hoping you would have said yes and then you would want to get together with them to show off your ring and talk about it, so I confirmed with them before we left."

"You're the best, Logan Michaels, and I'll love you forever."

"And I'll love you forever, Skyler Jones."

Epilogue

Skyler

This has been the most incredible year of my life, and for the first time ever I can say I'm truly happy. I came to LA in pursuit of a singing career and somewhere along the way realized my dreams had changed. I was offered the opportunity to record an album multiple times, but after spending time in Hawaii with Logan, everything changed. If I took a recording deal, that would mean tours and time away from Logan, and I can't imagine my life without him.

As soon as we got back from Hawaii we told our friends of our engagement and we asked Jonah and Sadie if they would be mad if we married before them. Being the great friends they are, they had no problem with it.

We planned our wedding to be in the club the weekend before it reopened so we wouldn't interfere with business. Mikey was Logan's best man and Sadie was my maid of honor. We spent the day surrounded by great friends that we both consider our family. Mikey made a speech about saving Logan's ass, and it was the hit of the night. Logan hired a wedding planner that had covered everything from decorations, to food and flowers, to making sure the club was cleaned up the day after the wedding. We danced, ate, and drank the night away. I even had a slow dance with Mikey without Logan losing it. We decided to hold off on a honeymoon since we had just gone on vacation. We needed to get Thrive back open, and we were going to have to finish the build on the new club and then start the hiring process.

The best wedding present ever was when the district attorney called us to let us know that both Billy and Troy pleaded guilty to attempted murder, arson, and bribery. They were going to jail for quite a while, and the DA promised to make sure that once they are released there will be a restraining order in place as part of their parole. Nick also pleaded guilty to accepting a bribe, but he only had to pay a fine and is on probation. He actually sent a letter to Logan and me apologizing for getting involved and explaining that he didn't know they were planning to set off a bomb in the club. I'm not sure we believe him, but since it was a simple apology we just threw it out and forgot about it.

Sadie and Jonah got married a few months after us in a delightful ceremony. I was her matron of honor, and I wore the coral dress she wanted me to wear even though I wasn't fond of it. Logan gave Jonah a huge bonus for helping him get the club up and running while we were in Hawaii, and he used the money to take Sadie there for their honeymoon. We talked to them about some of the great things we saw and did and showed them pictures we took. Logan even called the hotel and paid the upgrade fee for them to get the same room we did as a surprise. He's a wonderful person with a kind heart, and every time he does something sweet like that I fall in love with him even more.

This summer we opened Club Heat, the latest strip club in LA, and it's doing brisk business even though it has only been open a few months. I interviewed tons of choreographers looking for the perfect one to give our guests the best show possible. We wanted the show to be hot but have a classy feel to it as well, and it took a little while to find the right person. So far Clay is working out well. The funny thing about Clay is he's gay, though somehow he manages to know what's hot and classy with our female dancers. It's beyond me how he does it, but I like that I don't have to worry about him fooling around with my showgirls. I did tell him that if I caught him flirting with my husband even once he was out the door before he could spit out an apology. I winked and told him I was teasing him, but that part was only half true since I caught him checking out Logan's ass a few times. I still chuckle about it when I think about his reaction. I know it's probably mean but hey whatever, it worked and he's no longer looking at Logan's ass.

Picking dancers and staff we could trust was probably the hardest part of opening the club. We held two days of initial auditions and then narrowed it down and held one more round before we chose what we needed. It was impressive to see the looks on Logan, Mikey, Jonah, and Shane's faces when I asked them to sit in with me and rate the girls. They were surprised but tried to play it cool, and I'm pretty sure I wasn't the only one to have kick ass sex those three nights. Those boys were so worked up watching the girls dance I think they all ran home to fuck their girlfriends or wives. All but us, of course. Logan took me into our soundproof office where he fucked me twice; once bent over his desk, and I rode him once while he sat in his office chair. I think the only male not affected by the auditions was Clay. He sat there like he was bored, but since he has to work with them he needs to be equally as happy with who we pick.

I'm quite confident that day led to me being pregnant, though how I don't know. I never stopped taking the pill, and we have been having sex for almost a year and a half with no other protection. Apparently it was my time, because now I walk around the strip club with a small belly that's starting to show. Although I'm so glad I didn't get morning sickness, I'm tired as hell and I'm only four months in. I have no idea how I'm going survive the rest of this pregnancy.

Logan is ecstatic about the baby and can't wait for it to be born. He has been handling me with kid gloves. I have to keep reminding him I'm not going to break. At this point I just want to find out the sex. I need to start planning. We're going to turn the second bedroom upstairs into a nursery, and I want to know if I'm painting it pink or blue.

251

The best part of being pregnant right now is Sadie is pregnant too, so we'll have our babies about the same time and they'll grow up to be best friends, like their parents. She's having a girl, and I kind of hope I do too, although I'll be happy to have a healthy baby. I thank her all the time for pulling me out of the house that night, and of course she eats it up. She knows if it wasn't for her I may not have met Logan, and although my dreams have changed since that night, they may never have become a reality.

The End

Acknowledgments

I would like to first thank Mr. Mello for all of his love and support. He's constantly there for me, talking me through scenes or different chapters of the book to help me come up with the best story possible. He deals with my constant obsessing about my characters, plots, the process we go through to get a book published, and he listens to me without complaint. I also want to say thank you for all of your hard work. You do an amazing job of supporting our family so I can be home with our son and embark on this journey. I'm so proud of you and the work you do, so thank you and I love you!

My buddy DJ is amazing. Although he's only nine, he's constantly asking me about which book I'm working on or if I'm writing or editing. I love when he tells me that he wants to write a kids' book so he can be like his mama. DJ, I love you to the moon and back, bud, and I thank you for your patience with Mama while I'm editing and am focused on getting something done.

About the Author

Alison Mello is a wife and stay at home mom to a wonderful little boy. She lives with her amazing family in Massachusetts. She loves playing soccer, basketball and football with her son.

After having her son, Alison started reading again and fell in love with Contemporary Romance. Reading made her happy and gave her something to do when she had downtime. As she started to read more, she started to noticed things she really enjoyed in a book and things she didn't. She began to have ideas for writing one of her own. One day she literally woke up and started writing. She realized that if there was ever a time for her to write, it was now. She had a part time job to give her something to do. The hours at work were slow and she was bored with what she was doing, so while her son was off enjoying his friends over summer vacation she got started.

Alison finished the first book in two weeks and decided that she really enjoyed writing, so she kept going. She already had ideas in mind for books two and three, so she kept writing. That is how the Learning to Love Series was born. Somewhere along the line, one of my Beta readers convinced me that Michael, a character from Finding Love, needed his own story. That is when Alison added the fourth and final book. Alison hopes you enjoy her books as much as she enjoyed writing them.

She's so glad she started this writing journey and hopes you will stay with her for the ride. Chasing Dreams is scheduled to release in April and the first two books of the Love Conquers Life series will be out this summer!

Facebook:
http://www.facebook.com/alisonmelloauthor

Twitter:
https://twitter.com/alisonmelloauth

Website:
http://www.alisonmelloauthor.com/

Goodreads:
http://www.goodreads.com/alisonmelloauthor

www.ingramcontent.com/pod-product-compliance
Lightning Source LLC
Chambersburg PA
CBHW020359210626
46816CB00006BB/2039